# ONE STUPID THING

# ONE STUPID THING

## A Novel

## STEWART LEWIS

TURNER PUBLISHING COMPANY

Turner Publishing Company
Nashville, Tennessee

www.turnerpublishing.com

One Stupid Thing

Cover design: Erin Shappell
Book design: Tim Holtz

Library of Congress Cataloging-in-Publication Data

Names: Lewis, Stewart, author.
Title: One stupid thing : a novel / Stewart Lewis.
Description: Nashville : Turner Publishing Company, 2021. | Audience: Ages
    15-18. | Audience: Grades 10-12. | Summary: Follows Jamie, Sophia,
    Trevor and Violet as they contend with the consequences of their
    choices, navigate the drama in their individual lives, and search for
    answers to the mystery of what really happened that fateful night that
    changed their lives forever.
Identifiers: LCCN 2020053638 (print) | LCCN 2020053639 (ebook) | ISBN
    9781684425310 (paperback) | ISBN 9781684425334 (epub)
Subjects: CYAC: Interpersonal relations--Fiction. | Guilt--Fiction. |
    Traffic accidents--Fiction.
Classification: LCC PZ7.L5881 On 2021  (print) | LCC PZ7.L5881  (ebook) |
    DDC [Fic]--dc23
LC record available at https://lccn.loc.gov/2020053638
LC ebook record available at https://lccn.loc.gov/2020053639

Printed in the United States of America
21 22 23 24 10 9 8 7 6 5 4 3 2 1

*"What seems to us as bitter trials are often blessings in disguise."*

—Oscar Wilde

PROLOGUE

# Nantucket Island

The three of them stood together on the widow's walk, a small lookout platform accessed from the attic. The mist crept around the rooftops of the houses, and though they couldn't see it, the ocean raged in the distance. It was chilly for late August, but they were still dressed for summer. Laughter drifted up from the Beechman's party downstairs, but it sounded forced, almost maniacal.

Trevor, the tallest of them, had wavy dark hair and a knowing smirk. He'd found a six-pack of warm beer floating in an abandoned cooler, the ice long melted, and demonstrated how he could down one in a single chug.

Sophia, wearing her oversized Brown University T-shirt and her patchwork shorts, shivered as Trevor handed her a beer. She shared a secret glance with him, a flash of recognition. After taking a small sip, she said, "Tastes like carbonated urine."

Jamie, who also took one, winced at the sour liquid burning his throat. "Agreed."

"Amateurs!" Trevor yelled at both of them.

Jamie gulped more, then grimaced, putting one hand on his growling stomach.

Sophia placed the can on the ledge and gripped the phone in her pocket, pulling it out in one swift motion, like it was an extension of her hand. She opened her Twitter feed, taking an instant digital detour. Her bright green eyes fixed on the screen, and her blonde curls dangled in loose ropes over her cheeks.

"Hey, I have an idea," Trevor whispered, his smirk turning into a deranged smile. "BRB. Wait here."

Sophia's and Jamie's nods were almost Pavlovian. It was a thing; they always went along with Trevor. He took off down the ladder, singing a song that had been on the radio recently, mocking it with a nasal twang.

Sophia put her phone away and looked at Jamie.

"Your face filled out this summer."

"In a good way?" Jamie wanted to know.

"Yeah. You have nice cheekbones for a guy."

Jamie touched his own face, then pointed at her T-shirt. "You still gonna apply early decision?"

"Yep. I know we have two more years, but in my head I'm already in college."

Jamie snickered. "You were probably preparing for the SATs in the womb."

"Shut up. What about you? Still thinking of Syracuse?"

"Yeah. But their journalism school is crazy competitive. And I'm a white male, which ironically doesn't really help. I wish I was more ethnic, or even gay."

"Wait, you're not gay?"

"Only on TV."

A car drove by below them on Baxter Road, half an arm sticking out of the passenger window. In the hazy fog, the arm looked disconnected from the body inside.

"Plus," Jamie said, "my extracurricular situation is basically nonexistent."

"J, you run the student newspaper!"

"Yeah, but it's pretty dinky. You play the violin, you're a mentor for inner-city kids, and you look like a supermodel."

Sophia laughed. "Please. I wear sweats most of the time."

"Exactly. You don't have to try."

"That's really nice of you, but I'm not planning on walking any runways. More like the halls of old buildings with ivy crawling on them."

The beacon from the looming lighthouse at the end of Baxter Road broke through the fog in slow bright arcs, illuminating the two of them in brief flashes. During one, Jamie and Sophia locked eyes, and the ladder creaked. Trevor reappeared, presenting a carton of eggs and placing them on the railing.

"What are you doing, Trev, making us omelets?" Jamie asked.

"I'll have mine poached," Sophia said, taking her phone back out.

"No, we're going to play a little game." He handed them each an egg. "Moving cars. Windshields are twenty points. Roofs are ten. First one to fifty wins."

"Wins what?" Sophia wanted to know, still scrolling.

Trevor took out an Amazon gift card. Jamie looked away toward the hidden ocean. "Fine," Jamie said. "But you guys already have credit cards."

Sophia just shrugged.

Trevor spun around and whooped.

"How do we fall for his crap so easily?" Jamie whispered to Sophia.

"Dunno. Always been that way."

The first car that went by was a vintage Land Rover. All

three of them launched an egg toward the street, but the SUV was long gone before the eggs smashed onto the pavement, each yolk a yellow blob glowing in the dark.

Trevor howled like a sick dog. "At least we're doing something! You feel it? That's blood running through your veins." As he distributed the second round of eggs, he took on the role of a commentator, as if it was a major sporting event.

"Showing promise from Greenwich, Connecticut, is Sophia Long Arms, and right on her tail is Shorty J, who is not 'yolking' around . . ."

They heard another vehicle coming. It was a pickup truck. Trevor and Sophia hurled their eggs, but Jamie just dropped his onto the roof.

"WTF, Jamestown. You got a limp wrist?"

Trevor spat his nickname for Jamie with contempt, a bad taste in his mouth.

"I dropped it by accident," Jamie lied.

"Fine, ten points for me." Trevor downed the rest of his second beer and let out a sharp burp.

"Gross," Sophia said.

Jamie gave her a look of agreement, as if he'd never do such a thing.

The street below was quiet. Vapors rose off the pavement. Jamie looked across the shuttered, vaulted rooftops of the homes around them, some whose spires stuck out through the fog. "This could be an English village," he said to no one in particular.

"Maybe that's why they call it New England," Sophia said. "Due to the resemblance."

Trevor passed out the eggs again, and Sophia said, "One more and I'm out."

"C'mon, Long Arms!"

"Yeah, me too. This is dumb," Jamie added.

Trevor looked at both of them, slowly shaking his head. But then his eyes widened at the sound of another car coming.

An old Mustang.

The three of them got into position, like it *was* an actual sport.

The sound of the car got louder as it approached, and Trevor yelled, "Now!"

They all released the eggs at the same time, which sailed perfectly, like a trio of arced missiles programmed to attack a target. There was something beautiful about that moment, like time slowing down, until another sound came that made Sophia scream—a piercing screech of tires. The car jerked to the right, swerving into a tree with a deafening crunch on impact. Jamie jumped back, repeating the word "no" softly, under his breath, over and over. Trevor lurched forward, holding the railing. Sophia hugged herself, her jaw slack.

Then, a bone-chilling silence.

There was no more laughter from downstairs—just the tick and hiss of the Mustang's engine dying, the windshield crumpled inward, as if punched by a giant. The body of the car hugged the tree, and smoke from the engine ascended through the leaves.

The three of them stood there, frozen, waiting.

TEN MONTHS LATER

# CHAPTER 1

# JAMIE

As he walked around the bend to the more private part of the beach, he could just make out a girl in the distance. She was sitting on a bench in the middle of a long stretch of faded wooden stairs that meandered down from the cliff walk.

He didn't want to come back to the island and had been happy when his parents told him they were going to stay in Connecticut, but his aunt Gia was renting a cottage in Sconset, and they insisted he go and stay with her for the summer. Of course, his parents didn't know what had happened at the end of last summer. He had thought about turning himself in a million times. The memory was like a pebble he'd swallowed that only he could feel, deep in his gut. It couldn't stay there forever.

He looked up at the white puffy clouds smattering the deep blue sky. A single cloud could weigh more than a million pounds. They were nowhere near as light as they appeared.

When Gia had asked him to retrieve an old rowboat that had been abandoned a little way down the beach, he was happy to be given a mission. Anything to get out of his own head. Gia was going to put the dinghy in her small backyard and plant flowers in it; she was crafty that way. He passed a group of people laughing and playing Frisbee. He wondered if that could be him someday. Carefree. Weightless.

As Jamie got closer, he noticed the girl on the bench was wearing earbuds, and her long, silky brown hair was held up with a pencil. She stood and looked his way, but he instinctively turned away, embarrassed. When he looked back again she was sitting down, tapping her bare feet on the stair below her.

He reached the old rowboat, suddenly out of breath. He got in and sat on the center seat, then glanced up at the stately homes on Baxter Road. What was he doing back here? He closed his eyes, and his mind swirled back to that foggy night last summer.

"Listen, people," Trevor had said, after they'd all stood there in shock for who knows how long. "Right now, we split up and go home. Listen to me. Nothing. Just. Happened. The party was boring and we left, got it?"

Jamie had tried to comfort Sophia, who was shaking. She started to say something, but all that came out was gibberish.

Trevor grabbed both of her elbows. "Sophia, listen to me. You still want into the Ivy League?" Then he turned to Jamie, eyes teeming with fury. "You still want to be an award-winning journalist?"

Jamie had quickly swept a tear from the corner of his eye and nodded. Then he caught Sophia's glance but had to look away.

They had somehow made it downstairs, the party noise a blur around them. Outside, Trevor grabbed Sophia's hand, and they ran off toward the road. Jamie ran across the backyard to the path through the woods. He felt like he was being crushed; he could barely breathe. *What have we done?* played on repeat in his head. *What have we done?*

Now, as he opened his eyes and turned toward the ocean, two seals popped up out of the surf, looking right at him, one making a little barking noise. They had such human expressions—lonely, glassy-eyed, curious. He'd once heard someone say they were the dogs of the sea.

He got out of the rowboat and started dragging it by the bow, but it wasn't as easy as it looked. There was a hole in the bottom, so it kept getting stuck in the sand. He was about to give up when he heard a voice.

"Need some help?"

It was the girl from the stairs. Jamie guessed she was around sixteen. Olive skin and big brown eyes. Up close, he could see her mouth was naturally turned into a frown, so when she smiled, which she did right then, it was surprising.

"Um," she said, "I think you need to flip it over, because of the hole."

"Ah," Jamie replied.

"You bringing this toward Low Beach?"

"Yeah."

"I'm guessing it'll be a lot easier with the two of us."

She was really strong even though she was slender. Another surprise. She flipped the thing over by herself, then each of them grabbed one side and started carrying it.

The waves were small and rhythmic, gently caressing the shoreline. Jamie noticed one baby seal following them, but he didn't say anything, picturing the little guy as his wingman.

"I'm Violet, by the way," she said.

"Cool. Jamie. Thanks for this. Thanks a lot."

"What are you doing with this piece of crap anyway?"

"My aunt's going to use it as a flower box."

"Ah, how quaint."

Jamie couldn't tell whether she was mocking the idea or impressed by it. With the two of them carrying, it wasn't so arduous, and they got into a steady rhythm.

Out at sea, three sailboats formed a triangle near the horizon, their sails casting long, billowing shadows on the water. Seeing things in threes triggered him. He flashed to Sophia and Trevor, the widow's walk in the fog, the eggs sailing through the air, Trevor's devilish grin and cold eyes, Sophia looking at her feet, trembling.

"Something wrong?" Violet asked.

"Not . . . really."

The way she looked at him right then, with the fingers of the sun beaming light around her face, made Jamie want to tell her everything. But he couldn't; she was a complete stranger.

"You live here?" she asked.

"For the summer. I'm staying with my aunt in Codfish Park."

They stopped and set the rowboat down so they could rest for a minute.

"Cool pencil," Jamie said, referring to Violet's hair.

She made a face, and Jamie felt like he saw inside her for a split second.

"My dad gave me this huge box of colored pencils, like a hundred of them in every shade. I started putting my hair up with them a while ago, and it just kind of stuck."

"Cool."

Violet raised her eyebrows.

"Oh my god," Jamie said. "I hardly ever say 'cool,' and I've just said it like five times."

"It's cool," Violet said, not missing a beat. "How much farther?"

"Just up there."

They picked up the boat and continued. When they got to the small entrance to Gully Road, they set it down again. "I'll get my aunt to help me from here," Jamie said.

"Excellent. Hey, come over here. I want to show you something."

A few seagulls hovered above them, swerving left and right, to see if they had any food—or maybe they could just smell the wounded. Violet led Jamie up into the grassy dune, where the vision of the marshes on the other side of the ridge came into view, miles and miles of tall, wispy grass and small ponds of reflective water. The sun was gone, but there was a razor-thin red line tracing the edge of the horizon. A gusty wind flurried around them.

"It's like being in an old painting or something," Violet said. "Right?"

"Yeah. I guess."

Jamie had seen the marshes a hundred times, but she was right, they looked magical in that moment. He took a deep breath and slowly let it out, as if all those heavy vines that tied him down twisted free, the density evaporating out of his head.

They sat down and stared at the ocean, which from the top of the dune looked like a giant half-moon with a frothy edge.

"Wait. So your aunt is that lesbian in Codfish Park, right?"

"Her name is Gia. Why do you think she's a lesbian?"

"Well, I know it's a stereotype, but she drives a Subaru and looks like Conan O'Brien."

Jamie laughed. She did kind of resemble Conan, but with longer hair. "She was married once."

"Just a piece of paper, right?" Violet said, slipping the pencil out of her hair. Jamie watched it uncurl and fall onto her shoulders, like in a shampoo commercial.

"Anyway, I don't think she's seeing anyone now. She's really cool."

"Hmm. You *do* like that word."

"Seriously! I never say it that much. I'm a writer, actually."

"Wait, so writers don't say 'cool'?"

"Well, I have this English teacher, he says to avoid empty words."

"Like 'cool'?"

"Well, if you were describing the temperature it would be okay. For example, he hates the word 'interesting.' You can't say it in his class or he'll like, kill you."

"Interesting."

They looked at each other, smiles forming.

"It's not descriptive enough . . ."

"I get it." Violet's phone buzzed, and she glanced at it but then put it back in her pocket.

"So, you live on Baxter Road?" Jamie asked.

"Yeah, for the summer. With my mom and my Republican stepdad, who is kind of a tool. I like to verbally spar with him."

"Spar—now *that's* a good word."

"He's wicked right wing. He's even opposed to gay marriage, which is like, so archaic."

"Ignorance."

"Yeah, and he's also kind of sketchy."

"Really? How so?"

Violet stopped making patterns with her finger in the sand and shifted her body toward him. "He just is."

Her phone buzzed again, and she took it out.

"Ugh."

"What?"

"My so-called boyfriend, bailing on the party my parents are throwing tonight. Typical."

Jamie wasn't sure how to respond to that, so he just said, "Oh."

"So, you working this summer?"

"Yeah, catering. But I'm also working on some writing."

"The next great American novel?" Violet said, teasing.

"Something like that. Where are you in winter?"

"Boston. You?"

"Connecticut."

Violet started responding to her text.

"So why is he a *so-called* boyfriend?"

"I don't know. We have fun together, but he just checks in and out whenever he wants. It's not like I want someone Velcroed to me, but still."

"Velcro is made of hundreds of hooks and loops, and they thought the person who invented it was crazy."

"I'm guessing you know a lot of random stuff like that?"

"Guilty. Anyway, I don't know the guy, but he sounds questionable. Half of life is showing up."

Violet gave him a funny look. "Did your English teacher tell you that too?"

Jamie blushed. Busted.

Her phone buzzed again.

"You get more texts in ten minutes than I get in a month," Jamie said.

"This one's from my mother, calm down. Hey, I have an idea. Since my *questionable* boyfriend isn't coming tonight, you want to? Just as a friend, obviously."

"Would your parents . . ."

"Trust me, they won't care."

"Hmm . . ."

"What do you think?"

The fact that Jamie didn't even have to think about it was freeing in itself. He was sick of thinking about everything.

"Why not?"

She told him the address and time and then started jogging back toward her house, her hair bouncing as she made fresh tracks down the smooth white dune. It was a lovely thing to watch, but just like that, Jamie's mood soured, and the warmth he had been feeling froze up inside him. He was going to a party on Baxter Road—the road where it all happened.

Codfish Park was a cluster of cottages adorned with weathered shingles, old buoys, and fishing nets. Most had cute little names painted on quarter boards, like *Seas the Day* or *Salty Dog*. Some were so tiny they looked like they could've been inhabited by hobbits. Gia was shucking corn on the front porch of *Driftwood* when Jamie got back. She had on a purple cotton dress and her auburn hair was up in a messy bun.

"How'd it go?"

"Fine. The dinghy is right at the road. I'll need your help to get it."

"Great, let's do it."

After they reached the dinghy and started carrying it back, Gia said, "I didn't realize it was this heavy. How'd you get it this far?"

"I had some help from this girl, Violet."

"Oh great, you made a friend already?"

"Not sure. But she did invite me to her parents' party tonight. It's just on the cliff walk."

"Cool," Gia said, trying to speak his language. "I'll be making corn bread, while you eat oysters and caviar on Baxter Road."

They managed to get the boat over the fence and into the backyard. It looked sad, but had potential, much like Jamie's life at that moment. Could he really be back here and move on from everything? What about Trevor and Sophia? He hadn't seen them since that horrible night. Were they even here?

Jamie excused himself, leaving Gia to figure out the position of her new boat planter.

Upstairs in the shower, Jamie scrubbed himself very clean. He let the water get as hot as he could stand it and tried to drown out the images that still plagued him, flashing though his mind. Trevor's hard stare, Sophia's tear-soaked lips as she whispered her promise to stay quiet. The ticking engine and the smoke curling through the branches. The backs of his two former best friends running away. It was like a collection of photographs in a twisted museum of bad memories.

He dried off, slicked his hair back, and examined his face. He was pretty pale, but thankfully he had no acne. He put on jeans and a Fred Perry shirt, and then he headed downstairs where Gia was making a marinade in the small kitchen. He straightened the striped dish towels that hung on the oven door and aligned the whale-shaped salt and pepper shakers that were slightly askew on the kitchen table.

"You like order, don't you?" Gia asked.

He nodded. Maybe it was a way of exerting control over things he couldn't elsewhere. His mother said he shouldn't worry about how his clothes were folded or if the milk label was turned out. But he did. Especially now.

"It's nice to have you around, otherwise those whales would've stayed crooked all summer," Gia said. "Have fun tonight."

He looked at her, letting her simple request settle in. *Fun.* That was something he used to have all the time. The three of them, spending long, lazy afternoons at the country club pool in Greenwich, ordering french fries and chicken fingers on Trevor's account, playing whiffle ball with the younger kids. At night they'd buy tickets to one movie but stay for three (Sophia would always leave after the first). Playing video games at Trevor's house, an endless supply of sodas and fancy snacks at their disposal. Yes, fun was all they had. But then they made one mistake, and the world was tilted now. Slightly off-kilter. He longed for the balance he once felt.

The only way of avoiding the Beechman house on his way to Violet's was to walk along the beach, but he wasn't dressed for that. As he got closer, he tried to keep calm. *It was one moment in time,* he told himself, *almost a year ago.*

His English teacher had always encouraged Jamie to write

about his feelings. But there was too much emotion. The words would spill onto the page and not make sense. So instead he'd been working on a story about his neighbor back in Connecticut.

He approached the tree slowly, as if its branches might turn into claws and snatch him. The bark had grown back, barely showing any damage. One could never have guessed that it had caused a death. But when he leaned down toward it, he saw that someone had carved a heart, along with the initials RP. He felt a slow rumbling in his belly, and he realized his hands were clammy. They weren't the initials of the person who died that night. *So who was RP? Was it supposed to be RIP?* He shuddered as he took out his phone to snap a picture of it. Then he pulled the article that he had cut out of the local newspaper from his wallet. It was only five sentences long, which was something he'd wondered about since that night. Why was the accident hardly mentioned? Jamie was a newspaper editor; he knew this was not proper coverage. What were the autopsy results, for example? Did this RP person know what really happened? Could they all be caught at any moment? A car drove by, and he shoved the article back into his wallet and kept walking, faster than before, trying to shake off the scene behind him. The trouble was it followed him everywhere, a million-pound cloud over his head. He didn't want to admit it, but something had to happen. It wasn't going to just go away. He took a bunch of deep breaths, telling himself to try to relax and enjoy the night.

A man in a white uniform met Jamie at the front door, firmly shaking his hand. He had black hair with a spot of gray near the center of his hairline, his smile sweet but also slightly

cunning. He led Jamie into the kitchen, where Violet was leaning against the subzero fridge.

"Hey! I see you've met Ricardo. He runs the place." She
had on a pale dress that came down to just above her knees. A
woman Jamie assumed to be Violet's mother stood at the other
end of the kitchen island, swirling a glass of white wine. They
were both undeniably pretty, but it seemed like only her mother
knew it, looking at Jamie in a very confident way that made him
a little uneasy.

After a brief introduction, Violet led Jamie up to the balcony off her room, which basically overlooked the party. It was
being held on the back lawn, which sloped toward the ocean and
the steps where they had first met. Cater waiters walked around
with silver trays, and the guests—all in flowing dresses, linens,
and loafers with no socks—mingled awkwardly at first but then
started to loosen up. A few couples even danced to the big band
music coming out of hidden outdoor speakers. Jamie noticed
Violet bring up a picture on her phone—a man with unkempt
hair, holding a fish.

"Is that your dad?" Jamie asked.

"Yeah. He lives in California, kind of off the grid, I guess."

"Like, in a tent?"

"No, a trailer."

"Wow. Out of choice?"

"Yeah. We used to be this strong family unit, the three of us,
and then my father just took off."

"I'm so sorry."

"Yeah, it sucked. It pretty much broke my heart."

The air between them seemed to get extremely heavy, so

Jamie didn't pry further. He could hear one of the party guests beneath the balcony, a middle-aged woman who was clearly inebriated. She kept cutting off the man she was talking to.

"Can you imagine? Flying commercial is bad enough, but in coach! Just shoot me."

Violet made an agitated noise. "These are the people my stepdad, Lester, hangs out with," she told him quietly. "Some of them are chill, but some pretend they're holier-than-thou 'cause they winter in West Palm and have private planes."

"The crispier the collar, the dirtier the dollar." Jamie had no idea where that came from—he must have heard it somewhere in passing—but Violet liked it.

Just then, Violet's mother came to the door, her words soft around the edges. "You two want some snacks or anything? There's crudités."

"We're fine, Mom, thanks."

After she left, Violet said under her breath, "Just like her to offer raw vegetables to teenagers."

Jamie smiled, feeling a little more at ease. He was rusty when it came to this kind of party. Growing up in Connecticut, he quickly became aware that his family had just slid into the class level, that their house was one of the only affordable ones on the block, that his father was always striving to live up to his neighbors. In a way it was ideal, because with Sophia and Trevor he lived the luxurious life, but he also had parents who instilled in him the value of working hard to get ahead in the world rather than taking stuff for granted.

After the accident, all that changed. Trevor ghosted him, and Sophia transferred to a private high school. The three of them stopped meeting in the afternoons. Jamie kept busy with the paper to escape the shame and the loneliness. The only person he socialized with outside of school was his neighbor Grace, who was seventy.

Jamie was pulled out of his thoughts by the sound of Violet taking a picture of him with her phone, before he could even arrange his face.

"Hey!"

She looked at the result on her screen and said, "You're not telling me something."

"I don't go out much."

They sat listening to all the sounds of the party below, and it felt like something was lost, a tight string between them had been loosened. Jamie decided to try and pull it back.

"So, do you—"

There was another knock at the door, this time a man in his late forties maybe, a shock of white hair combed back, piercing ice-blue eyes. His shirt was canary pink, and he had a huge gold watch on. Jamie could smell cigar smoke. *The stepfather*, he thought. The guy looked like a cross between a distinguished CEO and a crooked car salesman.

"Oh, hi, Lester," Violet said, rolling her eyes.

"I'm told I'm not supposed to leave you two unattended any longer. There are some other youngsters who've arrived, so let's go. Time to partay."

Jamie and Violet looked at each other and laughed. Lester joined in, thinking they were laughing with him and not at him.

"We'll be down in a minute," Violet told him, somewhat sternly.

"Now that he's having a party it's like he suddenly cares about me and wants to show me off," Violet whispered to Jamie, who gave her a sympathetic nod.

Downstairs had now evolved into quite the scene, and Jamie tried not to think of the Beechman party last summer, which some of these people had probably attended. After standing for a while with some kids who were talking about a shark that was spotted off the Cape, Jamie's breath caught short and he could feel his pulse in his temples. There he was—Trevor—at the far end of the lawn, talking to some girls. He was using his familiar hand gestures, but even from a distance, Jamie could tell something was off. Violet noticed Jamie staring and asked him what was wrong.

"Trevor Duncan." Jamie pointed at him. "We used to be friends."

"Oh, Pretty Boy? I've seen him before. He's usually drunk."

"What?" This was not the Trevor that Jamie knew, the one who knew how to have a good time but always played it cool.

"Well," Violet said, "why don't you go talk to him?"

Before Jamie could answer, Trevor was walking toward him. Clearly wanting to give him space, Violet said, "I'll be on the stairs," and scooted off.

Trevor put a hand on each of Jamie's shoulders, gripping hard. "Jamestown! Fancy meeting you here. It's been a while. WTF? Where you been?"

It was a ridiculous question. Even though they went to different schools, Trevor knew where Jamie lived. He had Jamie's number. Jamie had texted him a few times after the accident, but he never got a response.

"Around," Jamie said.

Trevor's bloodshot eyes scanned the party, his arms hovering in the air, almost like he was floating. For a second, he seemed to forget that Jamie was standing right in front of him.

"How's soccer going?" Jamie asked, desperate to fill the silence.

Trevor scoffed like soccer was nothing. "Got kicked off the team after I showed up buzzed for a game." He laughed, really loud, and Jamie just stood there, stunned. He knew that he himself wasn't the same person since that night last summer, but this was extreme. After Trevor's laughter died down, he looked Jamie right in the eye, but the spark was gone. His pupils were glazed, his stare vacuous.

"Some party, eh?" Trevor said, the words blending together a little. "Lester Hightower. Big cheese. My parents made me come to network, you know, make connections for my future!" He gestured around like it was all a big joke. "TFL," he mumbled. "Totally Fucking Lame."

Jamie felt like something scary was going to happen, that Trevor was now dangling over some edge he couldn't return from. He decided to change the subject, reel him in.

"How's Sophia?" Jamie asked. "Still addicted to CNN?"

"Ha!" Trevor said, spinning around and almost falling over. "You really have been out of touch, Jamestown. Sophia Jenkins has a new name—she's now called *Slutty* Jenkins. Not very inventive if you ask me."

"What?" Jamie hoped Trevor was lying, but why would he lie about such a thing?

"Girls too, I'm told."

Jamie's mouth dropped into a loose oval shape.

"What about you, Jamestown? You look so uptight! What's up with the top button?" Trevor grabbed at it, trying to undo Jamie's shirt.

Jamie stepped away. "Quit it," he said.

"Aw, Mr. Nervy. What about Hightower's stepdaughter . . . you bangin' her?"

"Trev, why don't you sit down. You look like you . . ."

Trevor just blinked slowly and walked away, back toward the girls he'd been talking to. He started to focus in on the blonde one, but then he seemed dizzy, and she led him inside.

Jamie found his way to the beach stairway, where Violet was strumming a ukulele. When Jamie sat down next to her, she stopped.

"How'd it go?" she asked.

"He's like, a completely different person than last year."

Violet sighed, and for a second she seemed really grown up, like she was too young for that type of sigh. "You know, after my dad left, a therapist told me something simple that I'll always remember. She said the moment you want things to stay the same is the moment you screw yourself."

"Yeah, I'm far beyond that point," Jamie said.

Violet began strumming again and humming along, and Jamie started to calm down a little. When she paused again, Jamie asked her if she sang too.

"Yeah, I try to write songs, but they're not very good."

"Well, I could be the judge of that," Jamie offered.

Then, with the slow crashing breath of the shore below and the muted sounds of the party above, she sang.

*There is nothing I can give you*
*That hasn't already been taken*
*It has everything to do*
*With how you left us aching*
*I don't suppose you know*
*How I will go on*

## CHAPTER 2

# TREVOR

As the girl led him toward the house, he ignored the wide-eyed glances from the other guests. He tried to focus on her grip, the charm bracelet on her wrist with a mini silver surfboard and a red heart. What was her name? Chelsea? Darcy?

Inside, the powder room smelled so clean it made him even more dizzy. The girl handed him a cold towel, and it felt good. He sat on the closed toilet lid and stared at her while she filled a glass of water. He grabbed it and tried to take a sip but missed his mouth, the cold water shocking his shoulder through his shirt. The girl tried to dab at him with a dry towel and he snapped. "Stop," he spat, pushing her away. "Just stop!"

She backed off like a spooked animal. He wanted to scream, but then he looked into her big, innocent eyes and the rage inside him evaporated, leaving him with just plain hopelessness, and he began to weep. The girl just stood there, motionless, until he calmed down. Someone knocked on the door, and she called out, "Occupied!"

Then she walked over to him and smoothed his hair back, kissing him once on the forehead. Trevor pushed her away again, but gently this time.

"The thing is, you don't want anything to do with me," he said. "I've done a bad thing. Like, the worst thing."

"It can't be that bad," the girl said softly.

Trevor looked at her face—*the face of an angel* his mother would say—and felt a strange moment of clarity, like maybe there was a light in all of this, coming to him from this nameless girl. But then his gut filled with shame, and he told her to just go. She shook her head and said, "Fine. Good luck."

Trevor stood up and tried to fix his tie in the mirror, eventually giving up. Back in the hallway, he saw the Hightower stepdaughter, looking a little flushed and carrying one of those mini guitar things. He decided right then that she was undeniably hot.

"Nice party," Trevor tried.

Violet gave him a once-over and said, "Go home, Pretty Boy."

He laughed, but it was also a little sickening, because he knew he had become that person—the one that gets sent home from the party.

"Thanks for the top-shelf hooch."

Some colorful looking dude appeared and guided Trevor out the front door, gripping his arm. He smelled like dime store cologne. Was it Lester?

The brisk night air in the driveway felt sobering, which was good. He managed to get out to Baxter Road, where he passed an older lady walking her small dog. She gave him a look of pity that didn't register with him. He was staring at his phone, pulling up his last text exchanges with Jamestown. Had it really been that long ago? There were three texts from him back in September, all unanswered. The first one said, *hey we should talk.* The second one said, *it was all of us, you know.* Trevor winced when he reread that. The third one just said, *so that's it? really?*

He wanted to text back but it was too difficult while walking, so he sat down on the front step of a nearby house that hadn't been opened for the summer yet. He started to text Jamie *hey*, then *sorry*, then *nice to see you*, but he deleted all of it. Then he opened his contacts and scrolled to Sophia. His thumb hovered above *call*.

● ● ●

Trevor woke at two in the afternoon. He didn't remember much about the previous night, except going into town late night and partying with some rogue fishermen at the docks and falling out of a dinghy. He felt congested, and his head was pounding. He needed OJ pronto. He headed downstairs in only his boxer briefs, and Electra, their housekeeper, just shook her head at the sight of him.

"Where's the love, Ellie?" he said.

After swilling some OJ from the carton, he grabbed a tube of string cheese, opened it with his teeth, and went into the living room, plopping onto the plush couch.

He flipped through the channels on the flat-screen TV—a meteorologist telling an awkward joke, a woman crying on a reality show, a shootout on a cop show, someone yelling on Court TV, and so on. What did it all matter? We were all just marching toward a slow death, right? Nothing really seemed important anymore, like he was just moving through the world waiting to bump into things. There was no order, only chaos. He remembered being in Sunday school as a kid, clogging up the toilets in the church annex, stealing banana bread from the book club ladies. Even then, he loved the feeling of recklessness. But it always worked out for him. It never bit him back—until that night last summer.

He finished the cheese and scratched his scalp. Grabbing his phone from the side table, he felt a familiar twinge in his stomach. *What did I do last night? Who did I text?*

It looked okay, except there was one red number under recent calls. He had tried to call Sophia. *What?*

He swiped to his messages. His father had texted some dorky picture from his business trip, and his mother, from early this morning, simply wrote *playing tennis*.

He watched Electra fluff up the throw pillows on the ottoman. He felt a distinct sadness for her, that she ended up here in this house, fluffing pillows. Wouldn't she rather be somewhere else? He walked over to her and put his hand on her shoulder.

"Sorry," Trevor said.

"For what?" Electra asked.

"For having to work here."

"I love working here," she said, like she meant it.

"Okay, okay," Trevor said. "But what does it all mean, Electra? What's it all for?"

"Excuse me?"

"The meaning of life. Is it fluffing pillows?"

She laughed. "You have too much to drink last night?"

"Let's just say I didn't really practice moderation."

Electra started rearranging the magazines on the coffee table, which sat next to a stack of college brochures left as a not-so-subtle hint from his mother.

"Well, let me know when you find out," Trevor said. "The meaning of life, that is."

"Of course." She gave him a broad smile and continued to straighten up the living room. As he climbed the stairs she called out to him, and he turned back around.

"Whatever is going on with you, Trevor, don't hold it inside."

He nodded and then continued up the stairs.

"And put on some clothes!"

In the shower, he thought of his first girlfriend, Ashley, with her soft green eyes and delicate skin. They had been on a ski trip in Vermont, and she'd snuck into his room. In the morning, with the light pouring in through the window, she had looked like a movie star. And she was wearing his boxer briefs. Why did that turn him on so much? That time in his life—a time when everyone was counting on him and he didn't disappoint, when he had dreams and promise and pretty girls, when even in the chaos there was order—was so much easier. He had direction, purpose, and there was no stopping him.

Then there was the night when, after winning a big game, his father took him out for a steak dinner, saying how proud he was, letting Trevor sneak a sip of some crazy expensive wine. During dessert, his father was swiping on his phone. Then he went to the bathroom, and it was taking a while, so Trevor figured he should check on him. There was no one in the men's room, so he decided to just crack the door of the women's. Through that sliver of space, he could see his dad, aggressively kissing some cougar chick, pushing her up onto the marble sink. He shut the door and went back to his chocolate soufflé, which had deflated. It wasn't the first time he'd seen something of this nature.

One time, at a different restaurant, his father was on some dating app, right there at the table, in front of his mother. It was repulsive. He tried to distract his mother, but she must have known. She wasn't stupid. That night, Trevor had caught his mom smoking, alone on the back porch. He wanted to kill his father then, but now Trevor felt like he was just as much of a cretin as his dad. A guy died and it was Trevor's fault, basically. He stole the eggs, he made everyone do it. Stupid. So stupid. Was there anything he could do to make it go away?

After the accident last year, he'd tried talking to his father. Not about specifics, but just to share it with someone he thought really cared about him. But his father was always busy, or he would freeze up and shut down when anything became emotional.

As he dried off, he caught his reflection in the mirror and swiftly averted his eyes. He then decided to alter his state of mind, going into his parent's bathroom to steal a pill from the medicine cabinet. He took only half of it, as he definitely wanted to surf today. Aside from what had just happened in the shower, surfing was the only thing he looked forward to.

He dressed in board shorts and a ripped T-shirt, then went back down to the kitchen, where Electra was trimming some fresh-cut flowers and humming to herself. She seemed preoccupied and barely looked up at him. He grabbed an apple from the silver bowl and went out onto the porch. The clouds from earlier were dissipating. He began to stretch a little and noticed his Greenwich High sweatshirt hanging over one of the chairs. At the sight of it, he immediately remembered what happened last night at Lester Hightower's house.

He had seen the very person who had given him that sweatshirt.

Jamestown.

The nickname was coined by Trevor a long time ago. It was seventh grade, and they were studying the Jonestown massacre in History class. Jamie had done an oral report on it and mispronounced it "Jamestown." No one corrected him, including the teacher, until the end. Giggles had spread through the classroom even though the report was about a mass suicide. Trevor didn't think of the Jonestown massacre when he called him that; it was just a name that stuck.

He put on his baseball cap, grabbed his board, threw it into the back of his Jeep, and headed to the beach. Now that he finally had his license, he loved driving down the bumpy dirt roads that led to the south shore, how the crunch of the tiny rocks under the tires and the white noise of the wind made it hard to think about anything else but what lay ahead—the sun, the sand, the surf.

Trevor parked at the abandoned lot on the bluff next to a pickup truck filled with gardening supplies. He could hear the crashing water in the distance, and he closed his eyes for a second, thinking back to last night. The angel girl—she brought him into the bathroom, she gave him a cold towel, she was so nice, and he didn't even know her name. He'd rejected her. He felt his stomach drop, but then a slow surge of warmth ran through him. The half pill was kicking in.

The waves at Madequecham were the biggest he'd seen in a while. He peeled off his shirt, threw his cap on the sand, and started out with his board. The water was always a shock at first, but Trevor didn't mind; it made him feel alive. When he caught his first wave, it was like he was suspended between the earth and the sky, floating in some magical realm, the sun glistening off the curl, the graceful glide of the board cutting through the water. Then the rush at the end, diving off the board, knowing whichever way he fell the ocean would take him in, protect his fall. He had been so delusional, thinking that this world would protect him after what happened. His family's money, his looks, his grades, his success in sports—none of it meant anything after all. Some guy was dead because of him. A townie, which made it even worse. A person who had fought for his place in the world. A person who maybe had a child, a girlfriend, a mother still mourning him. He felt like a total screwup. Keeping secrets just like his dad.

After that fateful party at the Beechman house, Trevor had gone home and couldn't sleep. He kept getting up and looking out the window. Eventually, he put on a robe and walked down the stone path to the beach. The fog had cleared, and there were thousands of stars—like tiny diamonds scattered across the jet-black sky—and he screamed at them, at the top of his lungs. He was crouching there, like some kind of crazed caveman, yelling, "No! No!" over and over, sobbing. He wasn't sure how long he stayed, but it got cold, and eventually his mother came down and wrapped him in a blanket. She knew something had happened, but they never discussed it. It was just the way his family worked.

He had left the island a few days later. At the airport, there was a paper someone had left behind next to him on the bench, and he saw the small headline: TRAGIC ACCIDENT ON BAXTER ROAD. He read the article, and there was no mention of foul play. The only evidence had been the eggs–had animals eaten them? He remembered feeling a sense of calm before he boarded the plane.

He still wondered if that was the right thing, to pretend like it never happened. Because now their lives were indelibly stained with guilt. Even if they turned themselves in, it wouldn't matter. It was done. It happened.

There were only a few surfers out, but soon the whole area would be dotted with bobbing heads, the tips of the boards peeking up like whitecaps. He had adrenaline now, mixing with the pill in his system, giving him a perfect feeling, but one he knew wouldn't last. Even so, he tried to enjoy himself and *let it out*, like Electra had told him to.

While waiting for another swell, he thought about James-town and Sophia, how it had once been so simple for the three of them, how they didn't really choose each other more than complement each other, each one ticking off a box that made the threesome a whole. Jamie and his gentility, Sophia and her smarts, both looking up to him. But after everything, it was too painful to remain friends.

On his second run he cut left, up and over the crest of the wave, and launched himself from the board, catching air for what seemed like a stretched moment in time—slow-motion falling. It was what he'd been doing for a while now. Falling and falling, waiting to hit the bottom and face what he'd done.

That afternoon when he got home, his mother was in the kitchen going through the mail. There was an iced tea that Electra had probably made on the marble island, with a perfect slice of lemon set on the rim of the frosted glass, that she hadn't sipped yet.

"How were the waves?" she asked.

"Excellent."

Trevor grabbed a Gatorade out of the fridge and drank half of it down. His mother was staring at him, arms crossed over her chest.

"What?"

"Don't *what* me, Trevor. I heard you made a scene at the Hightower party last night. Can you please pull yourself together? It's the beginning of the summer, for crying out loud."

Trevor held up his hands. Busted.

"Well, if you think you're going to just sit around and surf all summer, you're wrong. I've told Alison you'd watch Bryce three afternoons a week."

"That little twerp?"

His mother tipped the lemon wedge into the glass and took a sip. She grimaced, grabbing some fake sugar packets from the glass jar on the counter.

"That little *twerp* will give you some responsibility. Keep you out of trouble."

Trevor made a puffing noise and said, "Whatever."

"And college applications don't fill themselves out."

"Mom. I told you. I'm not really college material."

"Honey, you had one setback on the soccer team. You still have so much going for you."

"I *did*, you mean. Past tense."

"Suck it up, Trev."

"You mean like you do with Dad?"

She shot him a cold look.

"Sorry, it's cool. I'll start doing them. Tomorrow."

By the time he got up to his room, lay on his bed, and hit the pillow, he was out. He dreamed he was at a big soccer game, warming up with his teammates, his father proudly cheering in the stands. During the game he dominated, but it was close. In the last thirty seconds, his right wing set him up and he headed the ball into the top corner of the net to win. His teammates picked him up and carried him, and he was laughing and yelling, the sweat on his forehead glistening in the sun. Then they went to shake hands with the other team, one by one in a line. Everyone was smiling, including Trevor, until he got to the last person in line. The hand he shook felt brittle, like bones. He realized it wasn't actually a person shaking his hand. It was a skeleton.

# CHAPTER 3

# SOPHIA

She spent a lot of time in her room back in Connecticut after that terrible night, staring at the ceiling. There was still tape from when she had stuck One Direction posters there. She pictured herself standing up on her toes and ripping the tape down, but never actually did it.

Sophia knew that everything she worked for was threatened now. What if it came out that she had something to do with it? She almost called the police in the days following, even waited outside the police station. She knew it was the right thing to do, but for the first time in her life she chose the wrong thing, and it felt like she couldn't breathe.

The guy had died, and so had her friendship with Trevor and Jamie, which hurt more than anything. They were like her brothers, the first boys to actually treat her as an equal.

Both of Sophia's mothers were driven like her, and super successful, but not very emotional. They knew something was going on, but Sophia didn't feel comfortable talking to them about anything other than grades (As), college (Brown), her mentoring (one of her kids had just got signed as a rapper), or the books she was reading (*Catch-22* for school, thrillers for fun). If she had to choose one mother who was more emotionally aware, it would be Jane, her birth mother. She was a bohemian type, a celebrated anthropologist, and more of a soft dresser. Courtney, her other mom, was a pantsuit-with-a-bob-haircut ballbuster, the CEO of a consulting company, and always worked long hours in the city.

One Saturday that fall, her mothers took her to Whole Foods, insisting that she get out of the house. Ever since the accident, she mostly stayed in her room. Every time the landline phone rang, she thought it was going to be a detective, the police, someone from the island who knew. She changed schools at the last minute, and didn't care that she was anonymous. She continued to mentor her kids and ace her classes. Still, it seemed as if the earth beneath her might crack and crumble any minute, like in one of those disaster films where they make it seem completely real. But that Saturday in Whole Foods she remembered feeling oddly safe, walking through the aisles, the products perfectly aligned and gleaming on the shelves like rows of soldiers at attention. *I pretty much had a part in killing someone, but there is now gluten-free granola with coconut and carob covered potato chips. There are dried mangos and organic peanut butter. There's the beautiful woman with the huge smile cooking artisanal pizzas.*

In an unusual gesture, Sophia took both her mothers' hands in hers. Courtney's hand was dry, and Jane's was slightly moist from the skin cream she constantly used. A mother with a baby in a sling around her neck smiled at them, and Sophia smiled back, swinging her mothers' hands a little, like she would've done when she was younger, then squeezed a little tighter.

In the next aisle, Sophia became self-conscious and dropped her hands to her sides, but she stayed between her mothers. She had always thought of them as walls, buffering her from the world around them, but she knew that was naïve. They couldn't help her that night on Baxter Road, even though they'd been only five houses away, drinking expensive wine and watching golf on TV.

At the end of the aisle, Jane picked up some marinara sauce and started reading the ingredients.

"She's looking for the S-word," Courtney said.

"Wow, you can't even say it?" Sophia teased. "Sugar sugar sugar."

Jane winced, picking up another one.

Courtney rolled her eyes. "We'll be here for decades finding every non-sugar product."

Sophia liked to hear them bicker. If they *weren't* bickering, she'd be worried.

In the dairy section, her heart stopped for a second when she saw the eggs. She put her arm around Jane and squeezed.

"Sophia-girl," Jane said, and the three of them continued shopping. Normally she'd tell Jane not to call her that anymore, but right then Sophia didn't mind.

They didn't linger in the egg section. Luckily, breakfast in her house mostly consisted of yogurt, fruit, and cereal, otherwise Sophia would've been reminded every morning. She still had nightmares though: the fog, the crunch of the car, Jamie's frightened eyes. They were happening less, but she feared they'd always haunt her.

At the checkout, she watched her mothers fall into their routine. Jane took out her recycled bags and peeled them apart, trying to do the bagger's job while Courtney stood firmly, one hand looking at her stocks on her phone and the other holding her credit card, waiting to pay. She always talked about growing up in Korea with nothing, but she looked completely natural with her black card and her blinged out iPhone.

As they gathered the bags and walked toward the automatic doors, Sophia saw him—Lyle, her former violin teacher, with his wiry hair and his lazy eye, and that purple water bottle he carried everywhere he went. Her whole body stiffened; it was a completely physical sensation.

"What's wrong?" Jane asked Sophia. "Did you forget something?"

"No, I just need to forget him," Sophia said under her breath. "Let's go."

She had taken private violin lessons with Lyle for a while last year, in preparation for the Spring Concert. He was always very professional, and Sophia never expected that would change . . . until one day it did. It had been raining outside, and they were alone in the house. He looked different that day, like he was hungry or irritated. Sophia was wearing cutoff shorts, and his eyes kept glancing at her crotch. She thought nothing of it at first. She had been dealing with boys eye-groping her for a while. Still, she could sense something in the room shifting. Then, as he was correcting her bow position from behind, he pressed his body tightly into hers. She could feel something on the small of her back. Was it his knee? She told herself he needed to be that close to correct her bow. Then he brushed his hand across her breast and squeezed ever so slightly. She abruptly stood up.

"What the—"

He coughed, clearly flustered. She pointed her bow toward his chair and said, "You can teach me from there."

She knew that whatever she'd felt shifting before was now fully shifted. She let him finish the lesson, knowing it would be their last one.

The next morning, she looked at her naked body in the mirror before covering herself with her arms. She started wearing Jane's oversized sweatshirts to school. She didn't even look at boys, just kept them out of her vision. It was like someone turned the lights off on her sexuality. She shut down.

At dinner the night after, Jane had asked her how her violin lesson went.

"Oh, Lyle is overextended," she lied, thinking of him *extending* his arm around her, grabbing her breast.

Courtney gave her a look, and Sophia could tell she knew something. She'd been through so many awkward situations with men, being a powerful (and beautiful) woman in finance. She'd alluded to it several times, along with a roll of her eyes. Sophia silently acknowledged Courtney's concerned look. The same one she gave her now as they left Whole Foods.

After dinner, while Jane did the dishes and Courtney was personal trading on her laptop, Sophia snuck outside. Normally, she'd meet Trevor and Jamie at the small park at the end of her street. But they weren't her friends anymore. How could they be? The park was abandoned, and one of the swings on the swing set was broken, the seat hanging askew. She couldn't help but see it as a metaphor for her life, which was dangling and needed fixing as well.

She must have been in some kind of trance, because when her phone buzzed it startled her. It was a random text from a girl on her street, Alexa. They'd known each other since they were kids but never really hung out. She invited Sophia to come over to her basement, where some kids were chilling. Normally Sophia would decline this kind of offer, but she was caught up on all her schoolwork, and she welcomed the distraction. Ten minutes later, she found herself in Alexa's basement with a few kids from her neighborhood. There was one wall that doubled as a chalkboard, and someone had drawn a penis-person, as well as the words *hell is here* with flames coming off them. There was a bowl of pretzels no one was eating. Instead, everyone was sipping rum and Cokes. Aside from her and Alexa, there were two Hispanic boys she'd never met named Reece and Skinny Joe, and Leeza, a quiet girl from down the street who was homeschooled. Sophia pretended to mix herself a drink, but skipped the rum.

After a few minutes, Alexa threw the bowl of pretzels across the room in a flourish and replaced it with an empty Coke bottle, spinning it. It landed on Skinny Joe, who was actually overweight but carried it well.

"Truth or dare," Alexa said. She seemed strangely confident, and Sophia wondered if it was the rum or her nose ring, which must have been new, sitting on her nose like a period at the end of a sentence.

"Truth," said Skinny Joe.

Alexa asked him if he peed in the shower. He got really quiet and then said, "Yes!" and everyone cracked up.

When the bottle pointed at Sophia, she knew she couldn't choose the truth. Because she was basically living a lie. The truth was something she feared on a daily basis. She chose dare.

"I dare you to kiss Alexa," Skinny Joe said.

For some reason, Sophia thought of Lyle, walking into Whole Foods like he was the king of the world. Then she thought of the boy at the fifth-grade dance who tried to awkwardly kiss her. How she pushed him away and he called her frigid. She looked at Alexa, who was really pretty, even though the nose ring looked like it might be getting infected. Her dyed red hair framed her pixie face, her lips moist from the drink. She thought, *Why not? What do I have to lose?*

Skinny Joe was clearly objectifying them. Of course it was okay for him to ask girls to kiss, but not okay for her to ask boys to kiss, which was so completely messed up. But the switch was flicked. Her head filled with lightness, and she blinked slowly, thinking, *I can do this.* She had barely kissed anyone before, but she kissed Alexa like her life depended on it. Her lips stung with alcohol but also the sweetness of the Coke. Sophia wasn't gay, but she felt free in a way that she hadn't since the accident, like she left her own body briefly and was watching herself from above. When they were done, everyone clapped.

The free feeling left her as quickly as it had come. When the bottle landed on her again, she sighed and said truth. As if Reece could read her mind, he asked her what her deepest secret was. *We killed someone,* she thought but didn't say. Her stomach churned with the bubbly soda, and she felt like she might throw up.

"I cheated on my Algebra test."

They all laughed. It was a lame lie, and it wasn't even true.

The game went on, but she wasn't really listening. Eventually she just stood up and bailed, saying she had to do homework. Yes, it was a weak excuse, but she couldn't say what she wanted to say. How many people walked around the world not saying what they want to say? Not speaking their truth? It was like acid slowly eating away at her insides. If she didn't do something about it, one day she would just evaporate.

She avoided her mothers when she got home. As she scrolled and surfed her usual sites in her room, she caught her reflection in her laptop and smiled, shaking her head a little. Back in her bed, she stared at the tape on the ceiling and thought of Alexa's lips. She dreamed that she was a stripper, like in the rap videos, and people were tucking bills into her bathing suit. Except she was wearing a one-piece, and everyone was laughing at her.

The next day she actually looked at her body in the mirror for a while. Then she found some scissors and cut the sleeves off a top she always wore and borrowed one of Courtney's short skirt she'd saved from college. She put lip gloss on, and lotion on her legs. Something inside her was sprouting, and it felt impossible to ignore. Maybe it was a reaction to Alexa and the dream, but whatever it was, it was real enough that when Braden—a senior who always sat near her on the bus—asked her over to his "crib" that afternoon, she said yes, as long as he didn't say "crib" anymore.

She texted Jane that she was going to be studying with a friend. Jane sent her back a wink, and she killed the thread. It was nice to have parents who were youngish, but when it came to this sort of thing she wished they kept their distance. Which is why she never talked about Lyle, as that would no doubt lead to a whole other unwanted conversation. It was cringey enough in Sex-Ed; going through it again with your parents was unfathomable.

Braden's house was new, she could tell by all the glass and steel. He held the door for her and led her into the spotless kitchen, where he got her a seltzer.

"So, you always wear Brown U swag. I'm guessing you're applying there?"

"Yeah. One of my moms went there, and at first I was like, no way, but she took me to the campus, and it was amazing. A breeding ground of ideas. There was so much culture, so much going on. They also have a semester abroad in Europe program."

Braden seemed impressed. "That's awesome. I'm sure you'll get in."

"What about you?"

He shrugged. Braden was cute, but Sophia could sense a lack of ambition. It was like a light inside someone that was on or off; you either wanted to move forward, toward something better, or you let life roll over you. Still, he had gotten the courage to ask her on a date, or whatever this was, and she admired that about him. She also liked that he seemed uncomplicated, a simple boy who had no secrets, or at least not a secret of Sophia's magnitude.

Braden gave her a tour of his house, which she thought was a dumb thing adults do to show off. There was a wine cellar that was heady with the smell of cedar, and a game room that housed a sad Ping Pong table with a ripped net. When they got to his bedroom, he sat down on the bed and patted the seat next to him, like she was a dog. Sophia laughed, and then he looked at her in kind of a gross but also thrilling way.

*Is he salivating?*

She did wonder what it was like to be as free as some of the girls at her new school, having whomever they wanted. So that's what she did. She lay down and let Braden touch and kiss her. He was gentle and went slowly—the opposite of her fifth-grade dance experience and of the horror stories she'd read in books and seen on TV. They hooked up and it was really great, until his older brother Rich came home with his boyfriend. Sophia and Braden had to scramble to get their clothes back on. She snuck out via the second-floor porch and giggled going down the stairs. Walking home, a little cold due to her new outfit, she didn't feel ashamed; she felt empowered. Why shouldn't she?

That night she had no dreams, or at least none she could remember, and she woke up energized.

At breakfast, Jane asked about Jamie and Trevor.

"We're at different schools now," Sophia told her, like that was an easy explanation. The look on Jane's face said otherwise.

"It's complicated," Sophia said.

Jane laughed and then cupped Sophia's face in her hands.

"When did you become so mature?"

"I'm not, Mom," Sophia said.

On the way to school, she actually tried to call Jamie, but it went straight to voicemail, and she was glad. What would she say? She missed him, but how could they just act normal now? She thought about texting Trevor, but she was afraid it would be evidence of some kind. Could she really just let her friends go? She knew it was inevitable, for now at least. Hopefully Jane wouldn't continue to push the issue.

That weekend, she went back to Braden's house. This time his brother was gone. In Braden's room, they watched some You-Tube videos and ate Pop-Tarts. Eventually, they started hooking up again, but Sophia lost interest in the middle. It felt like he was too inexperienced for her, like she had her sights on something higher up the ladder, a better conquest. So she took off, claiming it was "that time of the month," even though it wasn't. Braden was nice about it, and she was grateful for that.

The following weekend there was a costume party at one of her neighbor's houses. She wasn't going to go, but Jane convinced her to. It was a fancy affair, like most things were in her town. She grabbed a glass of fake champagne from a cater waiter when she entered, and looked around for Trevor, as she knew his family were friends of the hosts. Sophia was dressed as the Energizer Bunny (Courtney, of all people, actually owned a pair of bunny ears), and she ended up talking to some dude dressed as Elvis for a while.

"What is a gal like you doing in a place like this?" Elvis said, accent and all.

"Better than bingeing *Stranger Things*," Sophia replied.

"Well, can I sing you a little number?"

Sophia laughed. The guy was committed. He started singing "Viva Las Vegas," and they were kissing by the end of the first chorus. They found a laundry room and started writhing around together on the floor. Thankfully, he had a condom. While they were doing it, Sophia stared at a shelf filled with cleaning products and thought of the irony. They were being *dirty*. But she had been clean her whole life, so she had some mucking up to do. Elvis was sweet, and he smelled nice, and everything was great until his fake mustache came off in her mouth. When they were done she couldn't find her bunny ears, so she left them behind (Courtney would have to deal). Elvis walked her outside, and sure enough, she saw Trevor. He was being pushed into a car by some guy she didn't know, and he seemed drunk. Or maybe he was just playing around. Sophia hung back in the shadows as the car took off, and Elvis said, "Was that your boyfriend?"

Sophia laughed. "You think I'm the type of girl who cheats on her boyfriend?"

"No! I mean. Ugh."

She liked seeing him squirm. She supposed it was a trait that got passed down to her from Courtney, who loved her position of power over the men at her firm.

"He's just an old friend."

"Cool. You think maybe we could go on a date, like a real date sometime?" She noticed some pockmarks on his chin and a few nose hairs sticking out of his nostril. How had she not noticed this before? Do we just see the sides of people that are convenient for us at the time?

She gave him her number, knowing she probably wouldn't respond to him. By the defeated way he said goodbye, she thought he knew as well. Like Jane always said, *One and done.*

The rumors started pretty quickly after that night, and she wondered if it was because she ghosted Elvis, a way of him getting back at her. She wanted to talk to her moms, but it just didn't seem possible. So she decided to bring it up with her school counselor, who Sophia had always liked. Miss Leopold was a former Broadway actress who had kind eyes and a warm smile. She had been helping Sophia with her college application. Miss Leopold could tell just by looking at her that something was up, and she asked her what was going on.

"Why is it that girls are sluts when they're sexually active and guys are just rewarded for it?"

Miss Leopold sighed and said, "It's true, and it's disappointing, but your truth is all that you have—what you believe yourself. You have the power to rise above all that. I know it sounds easier than it is, but look at yourself, Sophia, you've got so much going for you."

Sophia could feel tears burning behind her eyes. If only Miss Leopold knew about the accident, the eggs, the person who died. If only she could tell someone.

"And I always say this. Sex is natural, and as long as you're safe and it's consensual, you shouldn't be ashamed."

Her success at keeping the rumors away from her moms didn't last long. Later that afternoon, Sophia was in the kitchen eating yogurt when Jane saw the crossed-out words someone had written on Sophia's notebook: *Slutty Jenkins.*

"It's just some stupid kids," Sophia told her, realizing with a drop in her belly that she could've been talking about herself, Trevor, and Jamie.

Jane looked like she was trying to form words but nothing came out. They had never talked about sex. Sophia had learned everything from school and from the internet. She knew that Jane had been with a man when she was younger and had some experience, but still.

"I kissed a girl," Sophia blurted out.

Jane tried to look nonchalant, but Sophia could tell she was freaking out.

"I'm not a lesbian though."

"Good," Jane joked. "We've got enough of those around here."

Sophia threw her yogurt in the trash.

"Do you want to talk about it?"

"No. I just wanted to tell you."

"Okay." Jane seemed relieved.

Sophia retreated to her room. She didn't dare go on social media, but chose instead to read the news. It was always reassuring to her to see that there was real tragedy in the world, bigger than anything she was experiencing.

She scrolled through some old pictures on her phone and stopped at one of Jamie sipping a soda at Johnny Rockets. She couldn't bring herself to delete it. She worried about how he was coping with everything. Of the three of them, Jamie was the most sensitive. One time, in eighth grade, he had shown her a poem, and Sophia had figured it was for some other girl. Jamie acted like it was, but she wasn't so sure. She told him it was really good, but a little sentimental. Jamie had turned red when she'd said that. She thought of texting him right then, but it was like a bomb had gone off, and it was all just wreckage between them.

She played her favorite Spotify playlist and started to write her college essay. Jane came to check on her, bringing her iced tea and crackers. After writing a couple of bland opening sentences, Sophia minimized her essay and opened her email. She started a message to Jamie asking if he was going back to the island that summer, but it didn't look right on the page. She reopened her essay document, erased the initial sentences, and started over. It wasn't clicking. She didn't want to write some inspirational positive platitudes about herself because the truth was ... well, the truth was ugly.

Her phone dinged. It was a text from her cousin, whom she rarely was in contact with anymore. It was a picture of her and her sorority sisters, wearing dumb hats and sipping neon-colored drinks. It looked like such a cliché, it made Sophia a little sick. Still, she sent back a thumbs-up and two hearts.

"You working on your essay?" It was Jane, back at her bedroom door.

"Yeah."

"What's the topic?"

"I don't know yet, really."

"It'll come to you. You'll kill it," Jane said.

She preferred her mother use a different expression, but thanked her anyway.

Opening the file again, she started to write.

*There are moments in time that seem small and insignificant but in fact change everything…*

When Sophia and her moms got to the island yesterday, they drove right by Trevor's house. His Jeep was in the driveway with a surfboard hanging out. All she could do was shake her head.

She was happy to be back, even though the scene of the crime was right down the street from their cottage. There was something about Nantucket: the salty air and the rumbling ocean, the sprawling dunes, being thirty miles out in the middle of the Atlantic. Even if it was fleeting, it made her feel untouchable. She took a long walk on the beach and collected some pretty rocks and shells. There was an older couple taking pictures of a seal, and some college kids playing lacrosse.

When she got back to their modest but cute cottage, the one they'd been staying in every summer for as long as she could remember, she placed her rocks and shells in a line on the shelf next to her bed.

Their dog—a droopy-faced chocolate lab named Bailey—grumbled at her feet, then was asleep in two seconds.

"How nice it must be to be a dog," she told him. "No secrets. No worries."

Jane came into her room to check on her. She had changed into linens and looked relaxed, already having a glass of wine even though the sun was still strong in the sky.

"There's a party at the Hightower's tonight," Jane told her. "I'm sure you'll know people."

The last thing Sophia wanted was to go to a party on Baxter Road.

"I think I'm going to work on my college essay."

"Gotcha. You know what it's about yet?"

"Whatever it is, I just want it to be honest," Sophia said.

"That sounds like a plan."

When Jane left, Sophia opened her laptop and stared at the screen. The cursor blinked, tempting her.

# CHAPTER 4

# VIOLET

She went to buy a ukulele because she hated them. Her friend Kaila was doing an experiment she called "embrace the hate." The idea was to do ten things you would normally never do.

The skinny dude with googly eyes and a woodsy hat in the music store tried to sell her a more expensive model than the one she was looking at, and she agreed just so she could get the hell out of there. While she was paying, he looked at her with a half-smile that was slightly unnerving. As she started to leave, the guy put up his hands and said, "Hey! What gives you life?"

"Excuse me?" Violet was trying to figure out the strap on the ukulele case.

"You should do whatever gives you life."

Violet was ready to dismiss his New-Agey statement, but something about the soft way he'd said it caught her, and she stopped for a second, really taking him in. He had a crumb of bread lingering on his beard, and she thought she could smell curry. She hoped it was something he ate and not just his BO.

"What gives *you* life?" she asked back.

"Music," he said, as if it was the easiest answer in the world.

"Gotcha. Well, I'll let you know when I find out."

The ukulele sat in her bedroom in Boston for a while and remained untouched until she brought it to the island last week.

It rained for five days straight, so she played it a lot. The chords were simple, and she had good rhythm. Plus, she'd been given vocal solos in her church choir in middle school, so she could definitely hold a tune. It was only when she started actually writing a song that she thought again of the guy at the guitar shop. She pictured him sitting in a room like her, trying to express something that was hard to articulate. She didn't want to sound like those pouty girls at her school, all affected, whining about their boyfriends with their guitars. Violet had been dumped, but not by a teenage boy—by her own father, which was kind of worse. If only she had been more perceptive and seen the signs more clearly.

Now, in her room in Lester's house on Baxter Road, tuning that stubborn fourth string and gazing at the wedge of shimmery blue ocean out the window, Violet decided to change the lyric about *how I will go on*; it was too dramatic. She felt a flash of embarrassment for playing it in front of that kid Jamie, but he seemed to like it. Maybe it was just an act and inside he was thinking, *Please, somebody shut her up.*

After strumming and singing for a while, Violet leaned the ukulele directly into the corner of the room and just looked at it.

*What gives me life?*

Violet didn't know. Her grades were average, and aside from sailing, she didn't really have any passions. She walked over to her desk where the infamous box of pencils sat, the one her father gave to her when he left. *Here, I'm ripping out a piece of your heart, but you can have these pencils.* They were, however, amazing pencils, perfectly aligned and in every shade imaginable.

She picked a color in the purple family and started putting

up her hair with it. It was lame, she knew, but it was the only thing she had, a way to take him with her everywhere she went.

The world felt so heavy when he left, like invisible hands were constantly gripping her, weighing her down. She had to fight to get out of bed, to simply stand up and be in the world. The whole thing had started slowly, with her dad retreating into the garage, which doubled as his studio, more and more. He used to make really expensive furniture—tables and chairs of repurposed wood he'd sand over and over again with super fine sandpaper, until they were completely smooth. He'd learned the trade from his own father in Colombia. He also made lamps out of curled copper that looked like Medusa hair. Violet had come home one afternoon to find him staring at the walls. The furniture stood in silent tableaux all around the room. Everything was completely still, and she got the feeling that it had been that way for hours. She remembered the chill that ran through her, looking into her father's eyes but not really seeing him. He was blank, hollow, completely checked out. That was the first sign.

She had tried to bring him around, and her mother attempted to get him to change his meds, but he was sick of taking them. Two days later he announced he was moving to California. Her mother pretended to try and stop him, but she was actually relieved. Violet kind of understood, but it made her angry to see her mother betray her father that way. To just give up. For a time, when he was making furniture that was photographed in *Architectural Digest* and selling pieces to famous actors, he was at the top of his game. Violet was proud of him, also because he was always nice to her and Kaila. He'd let them stay up late, give them extra candy, that sort of thing. She couldn't believe how quickly everything soured. One day he was there, and one day he wasn't.

When he gave her the pencils, she stared at the open box, the perfectly coordinated rows. It seemed such a contrast to what was happening. She had an urge to dump them out, start stomping on them until they were all broken. When he hugged her, he didn't squeeze hard. His body had gone limp. She waited until the middle of the night to cry, on the bathroom floor with the shower turned on. Her mother came and found her, held her and rocked her as if she was a baby, and she felt embarrassment on top of the sadness, which only made it worse. She knew things happened to people, more terrible things, but she really thought he cared about her enough that no matter what he'd be close to her. California was three thousand miles away. It might as well have been outer space.

She was practically mute in the weeks that followed, and in an effort to cheer her up, Kaila planned this whole weekend trip to the North Shore, but it all kind of backfired. Their Uber got a flat tire and it started raining and these worker guys harassed them. They got lobster rolls with soggy buns. The motel smelled weird. They ended up laughing about it, but it was the kind of laughter that precedes an even sadder silence. The next week she got a postcard with her father's address on it. That perked her up a little. After several days of pleading, she convinced her mom to let her go and visit him.

The flight was long, but Violet didn't sleep. She watched two dumb movies back to back. When the plane started to approach Los Angeles, it dipped through a thin cloud layer and revealed a sprawl of houses, a massive suburbia that stretched as far as she could see, millions of houses arranged in rows and around cul-de-sacs, some with blue rectangles gleaming next to them— swimming pools that from her height looked like they were big enough for squirrels.

She took an Uber from LAX to a deserted stretch of coastline north of Laguna Beach. As she got closer, the environment began to mesmerize her. The crisp blue sky and the electric sun beamed, the crashing Pacific roared, the windy cliff road twisted and turned, flowers grew wild everywhere in bright colors. When the driver said, "Here we are," Violet had to catch her breath. There stood her father's little mini trailer. At the squeaky door, he hugged her like he meant it, and she didn't want it to end. He let her inside the small space. There was a bed, a candle, and a few books. An old surfboard on top of some milk crates acted as a table, with four pairs of flip-flops lined up underneath it just so. On an old hotel baggage cart hung a wet suit, a flannel shirt, and that green coat he always wore. Violet kicked a flip-flop accidentally and he rushed over to correct it, and she knew, right then, that she had lost him. Even with the promising hug. He was just not the same.

The trip was still okay, considering. They spent a lot of time swimming in the cold, frothy waves and walking up and down the water's edge. They ate fish tacos from the truck down the road, and when the sun went down, Violet would sleep on her father's bed, him on a yoga mat on the floor. She wanted to say something to him, like, *Is this really how you're going to live?* But she couldn't; he seemed too resolved.

There was a woman who came over and seemed surprised to see Violet. Her name was Alida. She had braided gray hair.

Violet wondered if they were together, but she gleaned from their interactions that they were just friends. The woman had the same coloring as her father, but she was Native American. She seemed very nurturing and had a beautiful, kind face. Violet gave the woman her cell phone number and implored her to call if anything came up with her father.

He drove her back to the airport in his surfing buddy's pickup truck. At the curb, he gave her a flower he had obviously picked from the side of the road. It was kind of dented, as if it had been in his pocket for a while. Violet thought it was the most depressing thing ever, and on the plane ride home, she put it in the flight attendant's trash bag. That was six months ago. She hadn't visited him since, but once in a while she got a text from Alida, or a vague postcard from her father. She taped the postcards to the wall by the pencil box. One was a picture of a dog with sunglasses on, and another a vintage picture of a map that said *Welcome to California*. She thought they were cool.

As she ran her fingers across the postcards, Violet's phone buzzed, and she had a brief, flashing thought that it might be him. She knew it was dumb, but she still hoped the day would come when her father would call her and tell her he was going to rejoin society and come back home.

The text was from Kaila. As she was reading it, another one came in from Chad, but it was just an emoji–the smiley face with sunglasses. This after he bailed on the party. She honestly didn't even care about him anymore. Their "arrangement" was clearly expiring. It had been nice for a while, especially after her dad left, but he was a little intellectually challenged. She had irrationally hoped that he would somehow become smarter over time, but in the year or so that they'd been hooking up, his IQ seemed to plummet more and more. He was like a Panda—cute but dumb as a doornail. His name was Chad after all…what did she expect?

She went down to the kitchen, stopping short at the entranceway to watch her mother and Ricardo, who were talking and laughing. It almost looked like flirting, even though that was impossible. In addition to being her employee, Ricardo was her mom's gay best friend, and Lester was her ATM. Violet couldn't complain though, because Lester paid for the mooring on her sailboat, and just about everything else.

She took a detour into the library, which had wall-to-wall built-in shelves and tall windows behind a regal desk that sat at the far side of the expansive room. Her eyes scanned over the books, some of which were her father's Spanish-language philosophy books. At the end of a lower shelf was an old photo album from her parents' wedding. She flipped through and saw herself there, in most of the pictures, as a baby. In a few of them, her mother was trying to overly pose for the camera while her father focused all his attention on Violet. She felt a warmth rise in her chest. He was always that way. She could feel tears start to form behind her eyes but was snapped out of it by Lester, who sauntered into the room with a loud sigh. She slammed the album shut and slid it back into its place.

"Old photos, huh?"

"Yeah."

Lester's white hair was slicked back as usual, and there was something aggressive about the way he was looking at her. He wore a gold chain that matched his watch, more Vegas than

Nantucket. As usual, he smelled of cigars and that expensive aftershave. Or was it cheap aftershave? She couldn't tell.

Lester leaned against the desk and crossed his arms. "Violet, I know you don't like me, but I'm not that bad if you give me a chance."

"It's fine . . ." Violet said, wishing he'd just leave.

"The important thing is that you're happy and your mother's happy, and I'm going to do everything in my power to make that happen."

"What, you mean bathe us in money?"

Lester's laugh was guttural, and there was a trace of phlegm in his throat. Then he said, "If that's what it takes."

Violet sighed and continued to browse the books to give herself something to do other than look at him. Still, she snuck glances his way. He was plucking ice cubes out of a sterling silver bucket and dropping them into one of his crystal scotch glasses. Violet checked her phone. It was barely three o'clock. He caught her gaze and flashed her a greasy smile, and Violet had to turn away. He was either really genuine or kind of sinister; she didn't know which. That's the way it always was with him.

At the end of one of the upper shelves was a framed picture of Lester and Brendan Daly, a guy who had worked for him who died last summer. In the shot, Lester has his arm around Brendan, who is smiling wide. She studied the photograph until a strong whiff of Lester's scotch breath crept over her shoulder and made her wince.

"So sad," Lester said.

She didn't meet his eye, just put the picture down, feeling a slight tremble travel through her legs and up into her midsection. That whole thing with Brendan was so messed up, and she hadn't forgotten about it.

Lester retreated back to his desk at the other end of the library. Violet gave him a wave and a fake smile and then made her way out.

In the kitchen, Ricardo was skinning and cutting green grapes into tiny slivers.

"What's that for?" Violet asked.

"Oh, don't ask. Your mother's getting all culinary on me."

Violet reached over and grabbed a precut grape. The flesh was sweet but the skin was bitter. There must be a lyric in that.

"Can I ask you a weird question?"

"Of course, Babygirl. What is it?"

"What gives you life?"

Ricardo made a funny face but then relaxed. He had the looks of a soap opera star: full head of hair, perfect skin, pronounced jaw.

"You mean, like, what is my passion?"

Violet nodded.

"Probably my nieces and nephews back in Queens. They get on my last gay nerve, but I just love their little faces."

Violet liked his answer. She didn't have any nieces or nephews, just one cousin in Chicago, and her friend Kaila who was working in Boston for the summer. That's probably why she'd hijacked that Jamie kid on the beach. *What was he doing right now?* Maybe she would text him.

"What about you, Babygirl?"

Ricardo was the only one who called her that, and she didn't mind it coming from him.

"Sailing, I guess."

"Oh yes, you in all your glory, wind in your hair!"

"But I'm thinking about music, you know, just toying with it . . ."

"I heard you, Babygirl! It was very good, but it was breaking my heart a little."

Violet laughed. Her mother was lucky to have Ricardo. He was a gay cliché, but the best kind. She grabbed another grape and walked out back. There were still some chairs from the party that the workers hadn't picked up yet, and a stray plastic cup tumbled across the green lawn in the breeze. She could see indentations in the ground, proof that people had been there. But soon the grass would look fresh, after the landscapers came, erasing any sign of the party whatsoever. She went to the stairway and started on the forty-two steps down to the beach.

She remembered Jamie and the way he kind of limped on the sand. There was definitely something cute about him, but she wasn't going to go there. First, she needed to find what gave her life. Because the most favorite (and actual) thing that gave her life was a man in a dark trailer on a deserted California coastline, probably staring at the roof, the light from one candle flickering on his sunken face. But she was here, on the opposite coast, and in spite of missing him so badly, the world seemed wide open in front of her, beckoning.

As if he could hear her thoughts, a text came in from Jamie asking her about sailing. She sat down on the bench that was situated halfway down the stairs.

*Tomorrow*, she texted back, after checking the weather app.

The text bubbles kept coming up and disappearing, like

Jamie was having trouble thinking what to write back. Finally, he wrote, *cool*.

She smiled.

Another text came in from Chad that read, *sup*. "Ugh." She deleted the whole thread.

"Is that from that boy who came to the party?" she heard a voice say above her.

It was her mom in her yoga wear, sunglasses on top of her head, looking rosy-cheeked and happy. Lately Violet had begun wondering if that particular happiness was due to endorphins or actual chemicals.

"Jamie's just a friend."

"Well, that's good too. So, Lester said he had a talk with you?"

"If you could call it that."

"Great," she said, ignoring Violet's sarcastic tone. The small waves were redundant, like a sleep soundtrack. A tiny group of birds darted in and out of the surf like children playing. It was all stunning, but Violet couldn't shake another image out of her head. The one she saw in the library.

"The thing is, I was looking at this picture of Brend—"

Her mother didn't even let Violet say his name.

"Look, it was sad and unfortunate, but there's nothing we can do about it now."

Violet nodded, but she wasn't so sure.

Off the farthest dock, she raised the sail on her Sunfish, noticing the juice boxes some of the kids left in the boat last time. She had become a volunteer for the Boys & Girls Club and had taken the kids out sailing last week. It made her feel like she was doing something meaningful, not just summering with the one percent.

She could see Jamie walking toward her with something in his hand. When he got closer she saw that it was a small notebook.

"Um, I haven't been on a boat in a long time," Jamie said, gazing at her.

"I have life jackets," Violet said. "But you can swim, right?"

Jamie nodded and smiled. As he got into the boat, he told her about when he was six years old at the public pool and yelled, "Hey, Ma, watch me!" and proceeded to do a flip off the high diving board. His mother almost had a heart attack; she'd had no idea Jamie could do flips.

"So yeah, I have like a hundred swim team medals from when I was little. Mostly second place behind Trevor."

Violet stopped what she was doing and looked at him, feeling a momentary surge of inexplicable happiness, like maybe everything was going to be okay.

As they sailed off the dock through the harbor, Violet positioned the sail and the rudder at the same time, the rope in her teeth. She could sense him watching her. He took out his little notebook and wrote something in it.

She felt the most in control out there, the water spreading smooth and calm in all directions. Closing her eyes for a second, she felt the crisp air of early summer. When she opened them, she could see their destination. The stretch of land reached out like a long, lazy arm: Great Point.

"That was so creepy seeing Trevor," Jamie said as a group of seagulls soared past them in a flurry.

"You know, you're going to have to tell me more," Violet said. "You texted me that you were best friends with two people but haven't spoken to them all year and didn't tell me why. What happened?"

Violet tacked left toward the shore and then put her hand on top of Jamie's head so the sail wouldn't knock him out of the boat.

"I'm just trying to move on, I guess," he said.

"Well, if you told me, then we wouldn't have to talk about it again."

Jamie made a noise, contemplating.

They reached the shore, and Violet hopped out and pulled the boat farther up, with Jamie still in it. She always felt a rush in showing a guy she knew how to sail. The stretch of beach was rocky, with sand crabs scurrying around and skirting into holes.

"Something happened last summer. With the three of us."

"Okay . . ."

Jamie looked pained, like he was ready to tell her but needed a little more prodding.

"How about I tell you something first," Violet said.

He made a face like that might be a good idea.

"I stole money from my stepdad to send to my real dad."

It was true. She'd done it twice. She knew it was wrong, but it was kind of a Robin Hood–type situation.

"That's it?"

"Listen, whatever you have to tell me, I can keep a secret. It's like, what will be on my gravestone. It will say 'she can keep a secret.'"

As they walked farther out on the point, Jamie seemed to be giving in. He took out his wallet and showed Violet an article that was tucked inside it. You could still see the headline, but the rest had faded. She let out a gasp but tried to disguise it as a cough. The wind circled them in gusts, ready to sweep them away like in some fairy tale. But seeing the article, Violet knew this was far more sinister than any fairy tale. She stared at it, then handed it back with a straight face.

"Islander," she said, as if it were news she heard in passing.

Jamie put it back in his wallet.

"The three of us were throwing eggs at cars. I'm pretty sure . . ."

"Oh my god," Violet said, sitting down on a huge piece of driftwood at the very tip of the point.

"What?" Jamie asked.

"I just got light-headed. It happens sometimes."

Though she definitely felt at ease around Jamie, she couldn't tell him that she had an inkling of what had happened, or that Brendan had been driving Lester's vintage Mustang that night.

The wind died down for a second, the sky singing blue.

Jamie picked up a stick and started drawing in the sand at their feet, an imaginary language.

"I just keep thinking of all the decisions that led up to it . . . What if there was no beer? What if there were no eggs? What if Trevor went back to Connecticut early, like he usually did? And on, and on."

"That kind of thinking will get you nowhere," Violet said, readjusting her hair for something to do with her shaky hands.

"Yeah, well, welcome to my world. The world of nowhere."

Violet had to do something to calm the thoughts swirling around her head. She stood up, ruffled Jamie's hair and said, "C'mon."

As they walked back toward the boat, her heart was threatening to break through her chest. *Jamie had something to do with the crash?* If so, her original inkling may have been wrong.

As they got back into the boat and zigzagged back across the sound, Violet could sense they had crossed some kind of line. She knew his admission wasn't the end of it, that they had just opened a door into a house with many rooms, and that it wouldn't be easy to get out.

# CHAPTER 5

# TREVOR

Juiced on three espressos, he figured he'd have enough energy to deal with Bryce, the six-year-old kid his mother signed him up to babysit. He headed down the one-lane gravel road, which was really more like a driveway that jutted out into the bay, to a cottage on stilts called *Wait and Sea*. When he got there, Bryce ran out to greet him. With his thick blond hair perfectly parted, pressed pants, and crisp collared shirt, he looked like a miniature banker.

"My parents are doctors," Bryce said after they high-fived.

"I know," Trevor said. "Big whoop."

Bryce looked wounded for a second, until his mother, Alison, came up from behind him, ruffling his hair. She was super-hot for a mom, and Trevor briefly pictured what she'd look like naked. His face burned.

"I shouldn't be too late," Alison said, carrying a rolled yoga mat and a bottle of smartwater. "There's tons of food in the fridge. And what's the rule, Bryce?"

"No ice cream without vegetables first."

"That's no fun," Trevor said, and Bryce smiled. Seeing the look on Alison's face, Trevor backtracked. "But vegetables do make you strong."

"Ice cream has calcium," Bryce said. He was pretty smart for someone who probably still believed in Santa Claus.

"You have my cell, right, Trevor?"

"Ah, yeah."

"Okay. There's a puzzle that's almost done, and he can have thirty minutes of iPad time."

"Got it."

"Great, have fun!"

Bryce led Trevor inside the cottage. His phone was blowing up, so he let the kid have his iPad right away. The first message was from his father, texting from New York, asking about college applications. He deleted it. The next one was from a girl he'd named "Blonde" in his contacts. She had sent a surf emoji along with *what r u up to?* He wasn't sure who she was. The last text was from Sophia, and he felt his heart sink. *Did u call me?* she wanted to know. He started to text back, but what would he say? After writing and rewriting stuff, he decided to just answer her question: *yes.*

Bryce got annoyed by whatever game he was playing and threw his iPad onto the rug.

"Technology is frustrating," he said, crossing his arms.

Trevor couldn't help but laugh. He picked up the iPad and downloaded the TikTok app. At first Bryce seemed unimpressed, as if these silly people making videos were beneath him, but then he chuckled at one and moved closer, leaning his little head on Trevor's arm. Trevor tensed up at first, but then just let him be.

He thought back to being Bryce's age. Did his father ever show him cool apps? Or do anything with him? He took him to baseball games, Trevor remembered that. One time his father caught a foul ball that almost hit Trevor in the head. It was like sitting next to a hero. But then he gave the ball to some high school girl in front of them. That hurt, but so did a lot of things his father did. Looking at Bryce, Trevor wondered if he could be a better person. His father made truckloads of money, but all the money in the world couldn't buy someone a heart, or a moral compass. His father was basically a dickhead, and he hoped he wouldn't turn out anything like him.

The next video was a little racy, so Trevor swiped by it quickly.

"I've seen people twerking," Bryce said, like it was nothing.

The next video was of someone breaking a candy machine with a bat.

"That's violent," Bryce said.

"It's funny," Trevor replied.

"We could make a better one," Bryce said.

So it was settled. Trevor opened an account for Bryce, under the name islandkid6. He started filming Bryce, who just looked at the camera with a straight face.

"What do you want to be when you grow up?" Trevor asked.

"An anefesiologist," Bryce said, totally serious, and Trevor laughed. He realized he'd laughed more in the last half hour than he had in months.

He posted the video, along with a silly clip of a rap song, and said, "Now we wait for likes."

Just then, a text came in from Sophia.

*It won't go away*

Trevor went into the bathroom and texted her back.

*I know*

He thought of Sophia, her addiction to Twitter, how she was so confident without trying. How if any of it got out, her dream of going to Brown would be toast. He looked at himself in the mirror. It wasn't the face of a soccer star or a future college student. It was the face of someone who may have killed someone. He wiped away a tear before it could fall.

His phone buzzed again.

Sophia had texted back: *we need closure.*

He thought of that night, how the fog was so eerie. How he felt something bigger happening; how he almost knew.

*How?*

Sophia started to respond, but then the text bubble went away.

Trevor returned to Bryce and took the little dude into the pale-blue kitchen, which was a prototype of Nantucket décor: glass vases full of sea glass, painted wooden fish on the wall, a bread box with anchors for handles. He heated up some chicken fingers and broccoli. He put butter and salt on the broccoli, and Bryce seemed to like it.

"My mother eats things raw."

"Yeah, that seems to be a trend."

"I'm not a Neanderthal," Bryce said, and Trevor laughed yet again. The kid was pretty funny.

Trevor grabbed a piece of his chicken.

"Hey!" Bryce protested.

"So, is your mother an anefesiologist?" Trevor asked, not correcting Bryce's version of the word.

"No, my dad is. My mother is a psychiatrist."

"Ah."

"She shrinks people's brains. Not really, but it's just a saying."

"Of course, Bro."

Trevor once went to a shrink when he was little. He hated it. They made him interpret blobs on a piece of paper. He didn't last. Maybe he could talk to Alison though, even though she was hot and would probably be distracting. *A hot shrink is better than an ugly one, right?* Ugh, it felt like something his father would think. Either way, he needed help. He wouldn't tell anyone that, but he knew it.

He gave Bryce ice cream, and was actually glad to see that after spilling some on his shirt, the kid just left it there. It was reassuring to see him not act like an adult for a minute. Trevor had met Bryce several times before but never paid him any mind. How many people in his life had he passed by, even when they had something to contribute, something worth knowing? He missed Jamie and his reservoir of random facts. Jamie knew a lot of stuff, and half the time Trevor would pretend he did as well but secretly file the facts in his mind. Octopi see through their skin. Def Leppard's drummer has one arm. A group of crows is called a murder.

"What about you?" Bryce asked, licking his bowl. "What are you going to be when you grow up?"

"Still trying to work that one out, Bro," Trevor said.

"Well, time is ticking," Bryce said.

Trevor smiled, looking at his phone. The kid was right. It was actually almost time for his mother to come home. He checked the video on TikTok. It had fourteen likes.

"Wow, you're famous," Trevor said, showing Bryce.

"Being famous online is fun," Bryce said, "but I want a job that will actually help people."

Trevor looked at Bryce, who was now spinning his spoon on

the table. How did this kid have everything figured out? Was he just spouting stuff he heard his parents say? Either way, Trevor felt like a loser next to him. Presently, his only goal in life was to medicate and surf. He was pathetic. Still, he didn't feel judged by Bryce. In fact, he felt useful. And it felt good.

When Alison came home, Trevor tried not to look at the oval of sweat near her cleavage, soaking through her yoga top, or the way her tongue slowly swiped the corner of her mouth. She was like, forty! But that was the thing—forty wasn't old anymore. She looked hermetically sealed.

Alison thanked him profusely, and Trevor said, "No problem. He's quite a kid."

"That's for sure. So, how's everything going with you? Thinking about college?"

Why was everyone asking him that? Did his mother plant that question with Alison? Damn.

"Not really, to be honest. I'm kind of floundering."

She put her hand on his arm. There were two diamonds on her ring finger, and some Tiffany bracelets on her wrist.

"You know what? It's okay to flounder. You'll figure it out."

If this was a Lifetime movie, it seemed like the moment where she was going to kiss him. He even closed his eyes for a second. But instead, she gave his hair a quick tousle and said, "Go be a teenager."

*That's exactly what I wish I could do*, he thought. *But it's complicated.*

He said goodbye to Bryce, who was back on his iPad.

"He didn't use the full half hour," Trevor told Alison.

"We'll go with that," she said, winking at him. Again, was

the wink suggestive? He had to stop thinking like his father. Or was that unrealistic? The guy was his own flesh and blood. The thought made him feel like he was in quicksand. He took a deep breath and headed out the door.

Before heading up island, Trevor decided to go by Serge's boat. Serge was a French dude who had checked out of life a long time ago and had been sailing the world ever since. He got a check every month from his father's estate, and no one really knew what his father did to make the money. Depending on how drunk he was, the story changed—a circus owner, an inventor of kitchen utensils, a composer. All Trevor knew was the guy always had beer and he wasn't a creep. Hell, he was more of a father to him than his own, even though that wasn't saying much.

Serge's boat was an old eighteen-footer that was basically about to sink, with shit piled everywhere inside, but Trevor loved it. His whole life he'd been surrounded by order and opulence, and it made him feel normal drinking beer with Serge on his misfit barge that smelled of cigars and forgotten dreams.

"Hey, Sailor," Serge said to Trevor. "Want a cold one?"

It was how he started every conversation. Trevor nodded and then sat down next to a five-foot stack of *New Yorker* magazines from the '80s. Serge threw him a Bud Light can, and he cracked it open, downing half of it in one sip. For a while after the accident, he didn't drink beer, but now it didn't really matter. It was just something to alter his state of mind. It wasn't a cure, but it was a temporary fix.

"You know I could get arrested for giving you beer?"

Serge said that all the time.

"Yes. But I'd just get it elsewhere."

"Of course you would. How was your day?"

"It was cool, actually . . . I'm babysitting this kid . . ."

"Babysitting? Isn't that a girl's job?"

"No, Serge. It's just a job."

"Okay, okay. Good kid?"

"Yeah, smart. Like, maybe even smarter than me."

"Be careful of the smart ones—they'll turn on you."

Trevor had a feeling that was a lead-in to Serge telling the story of his ex-wife for the hundredth time, so he quickly changed the subject.

"Hey, do you think it's possible to grow up and not be like your parents?" Trevor asked.

Serge made what Trevor liked to think of as his conundrum face. Serge knew about everything. Brendan. His father. The girls he hooked up with. Trevor had spent many a night on that very boat, spouting his truth to the only person he felt comfortable hearing it.

"Not really, I'm afraid. But you can try to be better."

"Yeah. My dad's a douche."

"I know. Mine too. He always told me I was worthless."

"Serge, you're like, my only friend. You're not worthless."

"What about Jay and Susie?"

"Jamie and Sophia."

"Yeah, them."

"We had a falling out."

"I know, but I'm thinking you need each other now more than ever. Are they on the island?"

"Yeah."

Trevor felt for his phone in his pocket. Sophia's texts were fresh, at the top of the list. "I do want them back . . . my friends. But I'm worried I'm going to spend all summer drinking beer on a boat with a French castaway."

Serge started laughing, which turned into a cough. Then he lit the butt end of a cigar. The smoke reminded Trevor of the Mustang, twisted into the tree.

"We did it, Serge. It's permanent."

"Nothing's permanent. It just seems like it is. It's all an illusion."

"I hope you're right."

An inebriated group of people walked by on the dock, calling out to Serge but pronouncing his name wrong and laughing.

"Tossers," Serge said.

"Isn't that an English saying?" Trevor asked.

"Yes, but let us not forget, I spent four years in Brighton."

"England?"

"Jolly old."

"I'd like to go anywhere no one knows my name."

Serge held up his beer and clinked Trevor's.

"Hallelujah to that."

They drank the rest of their beers in silence. Trevor looked around at all of Serge's stuff. A whole lifetime of junk. What would become of it? What becomes of anyone?

Serge turned on his radio, which played some old crooner, singing about lost love. That was the least of his problems. He would gladly trade being lovesick for what he was now—broken, lost, guilt-ridden.

As Trevor left, Serge put a hand on his shoulder.

"Find them. Go to them. I'm here, man, but you need them."

"Okay, okay. Thanks for the beer."

"Nectar of the gods," Serge said.

"I thought that was wine?"

"German gods," Serge clarified.

Trevor smiled and hopped onto the dock. As he walked away, Serge called out once more, "Find them!"

Trevor looked at his phone. Sophia still hadn't texted back, so he texted Jamie. One word, just to see what he'd get back: *Hey.*

● ● ●

Twenty minutes later, Trevor finally answered the text from "Blonde," whose name was actually Mallory. It was the angel girl who had helped him in the bathroom at the Hightower's party. They decided to meet up at a bonfire on Surfside Beach. There were makeshift benches made from driftwood, and some dudes playing guitar. The fire crackled and sparked up into the dark night. The girls were drinking rosé by the can, the guys passing around a bottle of craft whiskey. He got mesmerized by the flames for a while, then checked his phone. Nothing back from Jamie.

Mallory gave him some tokes on a vape pen as they walked away from the scene to where it was just stars and sand. She kissed him, and he grabbed her ass. She was hot, and still looked like an angel, but he felt nothing. What was wrong with him? He pulled away abruptly.

"Sorry. I'm just tired," he said. *Of life,* he didn't add.

Mallory looked disappointed, but she also seemed used to

boys letting her down. The steely resolve on her face reminded him of his mother. When would the cycle change?

"I'm sorry," he said, really meaning it this time. "And thanks for your help the other night. I'm just kind of a mess."

"It's cool. Just text me another time, when you're in a better mood."

Her hopefulness felt hard to take in. Like there was desperation underneath it. Trevor wondered if there would ever be that time—when he was in a better mood. He made sure she had found her friends before he left.

On Baxter Road, he saw tents set up at the property near his house that always held events. He knew he could probably get some free drinks from the cater waiters that he knew from surfing. He parked and then checked to see if Sophia or Jamie had texted back. Maybe they had the same problem he did; how do you fit a world of shame and regret into twenty characters or an emoji?

The first person he saw when he walked up was Jamestown, in an apron, carrying a large bowl of berries. *WTF. He was a caterer now?*

Trevor didn't let Jamie see him. Instead, he went to one of the makeshift bars in the corner of the tent, snuck a whiskey, and observed. Jamie seemed to be working hard. He always worked hard—the newspaper, the coffee shop, now this. Trevor had never needed to work, and their imbalance had always been a strain on their relationship. He knew that Jamie judged him, but it wasn't like Trevor's financial circumstances were his own fault. His family was rich, but it just meant more problems. His mother and her chardonnay; his father and his wandering dick. He watched Jamie, wishing he could be in his shoes. At least Jamie had a focus, a distraction. *What's that saying about idle hands?*

Trevor snuck out before Jamie caught on. When he got home, his father was in the kitchen looking at his phone. He wore an expensive suit and mini golf ball cufflinks, a Rolex, and a fifty-dollar haircut.

"I thought you were in New York?" Jamie asked.

"Just flew in. Got a ride on the Worthington's plane."

"Of course you did."

His father looked up from his phone, which was a rare occasion. His eyes squinted a little. "T-ball, have you been drinking?"

"What do you care?"

His father made a noise and turned back to his phone. That was it, the extent of their relationship. Trevor was just a prop. *Look, I have money, I have a kid with good genes, watch him be just like me.*

"I'm not going to be like you," Trevor said.

"What?" his father asked, even though he had obviously heard him.

"Nothing."

Trevor got some water and headed up to his room. He started watching porn, but it just seemed sensational and empty. Some woman in her thirties was dressed like a school girl, and the dialogue was wooden. The dude in the scene had sweaty chest hair and bad tattoos. Trevor sighed and shut down his laptop, turned off the lights, and got into bed. Except he couldn't close his eyes. He thought again of the screeching car, the eggs sailing through the air, the looks on his former best friends' faces. Fear, shock, worry. He thought of sobbing on the beach, his mother bringing him the blanket. It was something. A warm spot on the darkest of nights. But there were too many images haunting him—the fog, the tire marks, the tick of the engine. Even Serge's beer and the cater waiter's whiskey couldn't erase them. Nothing could. Something had to be done.

He stared into the blackness, hoping sleep would come.

# CHAPTER 6

# JAMIE

Walking to work, Jamie thought again of Violet's lyric: *How I will go on*. It was simple, but it pretty much summed up his situation.

The catering gig, Jamie's second so far, was an event for the wine festival. Thankfully, he wasn't handling the wines. His only job was to replenish the fruit and cheese table if needed and bus the tables. There was a lull at the beginning of his shift, after everything was set up and none of the guests had arrived yet, so Jamie decided it was time. He texted Sophia:

*Hey, r u on the island?*

The responding text bubbles came right up, and Jamie's heart lurched.

*Yep*

Jamie shook his head. Was it that easy? Could he have been in touch with Sophia all this time?

*I saw T the other night*, he texted.

*How was that?*

Jamie glanced up at the main bar in the center of the tent. The bartender was a different guy than the last time. He seemed kind of nerdy, with curly brown hair weaving through his thin glasses. The look could lean toward scientist-geek or indie rock bass player; he wasn't sure. He looked back down at his phone.

*Weird*, he typed back.

*Can we meet? Tomorrow?*

Jamie sent back *yes* immediately, then put his phone away. He walked up to the main bar. Mr. Cool Nerd smiled, reached out his hand. Firm grip. Light blue eyes behind his glasses.

"Hey, I'm Cameron," he said. "You?"

"Jamie."

The bartenders got to wear regular clothes, while Jamie was stuck in the cater waiter uniform: black pants, white shirt, black apron. Cameron had on a vintage sweater and khakis, a couple of rope bracelets on his left wrist.

"I didn't see you at the last event," Jamie said.

"Yeah, I actually work in Boston. I'm just helping out a friend for a bit."

"You mean you're not trying to be a career bartender?"

Cameron laughed, and it gave Jamie a warm rush. He wasn't sure if it was because Sophia wanted to meet or that Trevor had actually texted him, but he was starting to feel a little more like himself—turned on, less muted.

"What about you? The fruit and cheese guy?"

"Living the dream."

Cameron started to poke at the chunk of ice in the bin below him, to separate it. He seemed familiar, and Jamie couldn't pinpoint why. Definitely older.

"You in college?"

"Yeah, gonna be a sophomore."

Jamie calculated what age that made him. Twenty?

"Cool, I'm eternally in high school it seems. Gonna be a junior."

"Oh shit," Cameron said.

"What?"

"I just realized I left my keys in my car. Can you watch the bar for two minutes?"

"Sure, but—"

"Be right back!"

While Cameron ran out to Baxter Road, Jamie took out his phone. There was a text from Violet.

*I knew Brendan. We should talk.*

Jamie's knees almost buckled, seeing the name on his phone: *Brendan.*

*At work talk soon,* Jamie texted back.

"No texting, Bud." It was Pete, his boss.

"Oh, sorry. Cameron just had to go get his keys."

"Gotcha."

Jamie made himself busy with chipping the ice.

"So," Pete said, "you'll see a guy in a colorful suit, can't miss him. His name is Mr. Enlin. He drinks only Pellegrino. Keep him topped off. He owns like, all of Pittsburgh."

"Good to know," Jamie said.

"And his wife, get this, she'll tell you how many homes she has within the first second of meeting her. Just act impressed. Anyway, you'd think his money would be enough. Her family name is Lays, like the potato chips!"

Jamie smiled. He knew Pete from prior summers. He was always hanging around the docks in town, jabbering on. Jamie was thankful when Cameron returned.

"Look who the shark dragged in," Pete said.

"Sorry! I know there's like, no crime here, but if it's going to happen to anyone, it's me. Things come in threes."

"Oh. What were the other two?" Pete asked.

"My sister lost her baby, and my cat ran away."

"Wow."

"Waiting for the third thing," Cameron replied, smiling at Jamie.

Jamie made sure Mr. Enlin had his Pellegrino, and the Lays woman did, in fact, tell him about her homes. Palm Beach, Aspen, Paris. The owner of the winery that was sponsoring the event—a loud Italian guy—gave a speech, but Jamie wasn't listening. Instead he went to the bathroom and texted Trevor back the same word Trevor had texted him: *hey*.

When the guests started leaving, Jamie had more work to do. He started helping the guys fold up chairs and the DJ load out his equipment. It was the kind of job where you stayed around helping until everything was done. When it was, Pete gave them each an extra fifty dollars and said, "That'll get you a burger on this island, maybe a Coke too."

Cameron offered to give Jamie a ride home. Even though it was a short walk, Jamie was tired enough to say yes.

The car was a Range Rover, apparently loaned to him by his friend's dad. It was smooth and shiny inside, perfectly detailed. Jamie felt at ease. Cameron put on ACK FM, which was playing a Billie Eilish song.

"Codfish Park," Jamie said.

"Taxi in service."

As they drove, Cameron tapped his hands on the steering wheel to the beat and half hummed along.

"Since when did pop stars start to mumble?"

"I kind of like her vibe."

*I like yours*, Jamie didn't say.

Cameron pulled up to the house, the wheels crunching the crushed shell driveway. "It was cool to meet you," he said.

"Thanks."

*Thanks?* Jamie felt his IQ plummeting by the second.

Cameron fixed his hair a little in the rearview.

"Are you in a band or something?" Jamie asked.

"No, but I'll take that as a compliment. I'm a writer."

"Me too!" Jamie blurted out. He then proceeded to turn bright red.

"Hey, this is going to sound weird," Cameron said, turning off the engine. "But maybe you're the third thing."

"The third catastrophe?"

"No, a good one, if that's possible."

The silence in the car got louder. They smiled at each other, and the next thing you know Cameron was trying to kiss him. Jamie backed away.

"Shit. Sorry," Cameron said.

"No, no, it's fine, I just wasn't expecting . . ."

"It's totally cool, it's just . . . you seemed like someone who wanted to be kissed."

"I am! I do, I just . . . never, you know . . ."

"Got it. No problem. I'm gonna be at the next couple events. I'll see you then?"

"Yes. Thanks for the . . ."

"Awkward kiss fail? Any time!"

"I was going to say thanks for the ride."

"That too."

They smiled at each other again, and then Jamie turned to open the door.

When he got inside the cottage, he was thankful Gia wasn't there. He couldn't talk to her right then. He needed to process what had just happened. He went to his room and lay on his bed, looking at the ceiling. Why did he back away? He wanted to kiss Cameron, didn't he? Or was he just feeling a connection? It was definitely something. But he wasn't gay. The only time he ever even thought about it was in sixth grade, with his friend Shane.

Jamie had met Shane at the beginning of the year, when they had to cut up a frog in Biology. Shane cracked up when Jamie dry-heaved at the sight of the frog's innards. From then on, they hit it off. They tried cigarettes by the train tracks, snuck into R-rated movies, and attempted to drink his father's eighty-year-old scotch. Shane was someone who didn't play by the rules, and that thrilled Jamie, as he'd always been the good boy.

Shane lived in a huge mansion, practically alone, because his parents were never around. One night, as they were jumping off the third-floor landing onto mattresses they'd stacked in the living room, a massive thunderstorm rolled in. By the time it got dark out, they were still jumping but getting exhausted. Shane's parents were out at a party in the city and wouldn't be home until really late. Shane told Jamie that he hated being alone so late and there was no way Jamie should walk home in the rain, that he should just stay the night. Jamie called his mom and okayed it with her, lying that there was adult supervision. They ended up in the TV room watching *X-Men* together on the huge leather couch. During a tender moment of the film, Jamie tried to hide his tears. When the movie was over, the storm raged harder. Jamie remembered feeling scared—like, really scared. The wind was whipping the trees against the house, and the power went out twice. The third time it went out, it didn't come back. Shane lit a candle, put it on the coffee table, and they talked in whispery voices about school, sports, and their annoying parents.

Shane was different from anyone else Jamie had known, so he wasn't surprised when he leaned closer to the candle, the light dappling his face, and told Jamie that he loved him.

"Not like *love* love," Shane added, "but you're cool."

Jamie felt this weird sensation, like he wanted to be wrapped in a blanket or something. Shane lay down on the couch, and even in that dim light Jamie thought he could actually see his heartbeat beneath his sweatshirt. Jamie lay down too, facing the other way, their feet flicking against each other. Jamie stared at the gilded lamp and the dancing candlelight for a long time before he finally fell asleep. The weird thing was, when he woke up in the morning, Shane was on the same side of the couch, facing him in a sort of half embrace. Jamie got up without waking Shane and snuck out, as if he were tiptoeing away from a crime.

Outside, it looked like Armageddon. There were trees and telephone wires down, and the streets were deserted. He walked home, trying to take in what had just happened. When he got to his room, he wrote some words down.

*The storm is our truth teller, the wind is our sin*
*Where do you end, and where do I begin?*
*You act so open, like there's no code to crack*
*Like you'd never say I love you*
*Just to hear me say it back*

Now, he realized why Cameron looked familiar. He reminded him of Shane—or, more importantly, how that experience made him feel. He wanted the kiss, but felt it was somehow dangerous. He knew girls kissed each other all the time, but it just didn't happen that much with guys. Was he afraid of losing his masculinity? What the hell was all that bullshit patriarchy stuff anyway? Was it true that being sexually fluid is human beings' most natural state? (He had heard that on a podcast one time.)

Jamie was restless. He could never sleep now, even though he was super tired. He texted Violet, and she responded right away. They met twenty minutes later at the Sconset rotary and started walking toward Low Beach. There were a ton of stars, way more than he'd ever seen in Connecticut. She talked about her "creepy" stepfather and her "dumb" boyfriend, but Jamie was distracted, still reeling from what had happened, or rather didn't happen, in Cameron's car.

They climbed up the lifeguard stand and sat together, looking out at the dark, shimmering sea. Violet looked different somehow. Was it makeup?

"So, have you talked to your friends?" Violet asked.

"We've been texting a little."

"And . . ."

"I don't know. I feel like we have to reconnect, you know? If any of this is going to really go away."

"Well, I think something else was going on that night Brendan died. He was at my house right before."

"What? Why?"

"He worked for my stepfather."

"That's crazy. I mean I know it's a small island, but the fact that I just met you on the beach and we have that connection?"

"Yeah. If you want to learn more, you need to talk to Rosa Perez."

Where had he heard that name?

"Oh my god . . . the initials on the tree."

"What?"

"RP. She must have carved her initials into it."

"She lives on Martha's Vineyard now."

"You know where?"

"No, but I know where she works. Assuming she still works there."

The waves came in, one after another. The sound, along with Violet's news, made Jamie feel hopeful.

"I'm going to see Sophia tomorrow. Maybe we can go find Rosa."

"If you do, ask her about Brendan and my stepfather. There was something going on, I know it. My mother just puts blinders on, and Ricardo is very loyal to her, but I know they both know something."

"Cool. I mean not cool, you know . . ."

She laughed a little, and the moon shone in her dark eyes.

In an act of impulse Jamie moved in to kiss her, and she laughed again. That was probably the worst reaction ever. He felt like a complete loser. Is that what Cameron had felt like earlier?

"Jamie, it's not like that."

"Not like what?"

"You're nice, and I like you, but I'm not trying to hook up with you."

"Okay, okay. I'm stupid. I'm sorry."

"It's fine."

Jamie thought of Trevor, who could basically kiss any girl he wanted. He had swagger, an undeniable masculine confidence. He'd always envied that in his former friend. Jamie once shamefully thought being in close proximity to him would bring this gift upon himself, but he always ranked slightly under Trevor's bar—in looks, sports, even in grades. Jamie excelled in school, but he had to really try. It killed him that Trevor could get good grades without even studying. The only subject where Jamie clearly outshined him was English. Jamie had even written a few papers for Trevor.

He now had two epic fail kiss attempts tonight, and was left baffled. He should have let Cameron kiss him. Why not? He also should have thought it out before trying to kiss Violet. He felt a wave of tiredness run through him.

"I gotta go," he said.

"Me too. Keep me posted."

They climbed back down to the sand and hugged before walking in opposite directions.

As Jamie walked home, his mind swirled with thoughts. Who was he? Someone who wanted to kiss a guy but realized it too late, wanted to kiss a girl but couldn't read the signs. What a mess.

Aunt Gia was reading a book downstairs when he got home. She could sense that he didn't want to talk, and he was grateful for that. She told him she had to leave early the next morning, but there was cereal and fruit for him.

"Thanks," he said.

When he got into bed, his phone buzzed. It was a Boston area code, and he realized right away it was Cameron. Jamie had given him his number before he left his car.

*Are you recovering from the GREAT KISS THAT NEVER WAS?*

Jamie sent back a laughing emoji.

*I'm not so great at reading signs*

*Me neither. Where are you?* Jamie typed.

*Dunkin donuts . . . dinner of champions*

☺

*There's a woman behind the counter with hair so big she could hide a child in it.*

*Lol. What color is it? The hair?*

*A super natural shade of peach.*

*Eww*

*But it matches her spray tan*

☺

*She called me honey like twelve times*

*I would too,* Jamie typed, but then changed it to, *maybe 'cause you're sweet*

*Not sure, but this caramel latte is Yum*

There was a space of time where both of them were typing but neither hit send. Then finally, Cameron did.

*Yeah, sorry if I was too forward tho*

*It's fine!* Jamie typed but then got rid of the explanation point. Then he added another line: *I was just not expecting it*

*I take it you like expecting things,* Cameron typed back.

*Kind of*

*Okay, next time I kiss you, I'll send you a memo*

*Lol*

*Where are you?*

*In bed*

Cameron sent a blushing face.

*Don't worry, I have pajamas on*, Jamie sent, immediately regretting it.

*Hmm . . . what kind?*

*They just have stripes*

*Stripes are good, but I'm thinking you're not a straight line kind of guy*

Now Jamie was blushing. *TBD*, he sent back.

*Sweet dreams*

*I'd say the same, but I think your caramel latte has you covered*

He sent back an emoji with a winking heart eye, and Jamie stared at it for a while, running his finger over it.

He turned his phone off and shut out the light. In spite of everything, he was smiling in the dark. Amid all the chaos and confusion there was optimism, the same feeling he got when his friends started texting again, when Violet told him that Brendan's death might have been related to her stepfather. They were little bits of hope, and together it was enough to make him relax and fall into a deep sleep.

**o o o**

The next day he met Sophia at the lighthouse. She was prettier than ever, and Jamie thought about what Trevor had said. *Slutty Jenkins.* Were they just rumors?

"I missed you," Jamie said after they hugged.

"Same," she replied. "It's been a pretty shit year."

"Yeah. I thought about contacting you . . ."

"Me too. I actually wrote emails but never sent them."

"How are your moms?"

"Fine. The same, I guess."

There was a silence between them, and Jamie knew it would be easy to be friends again. It felt like they already were. As if to reassure this thought, Sophia blurted out a confession.

"I'm not a virgin anymore, so there's that."

"Cool." Jamie tried to be nonchalant. He was definitely behind as far as virginity was concerned. He'd never been past second base. It was beyond embarrassing.

"I guess. I also kissed a girl."

"What?"

"It was just a truth or dare thing."

"Ah."

They sat down on the top of the bluff in the long grass. The grass was itchy, but Jamie didn't care. He was so happy to be hanging out with Sophia.

"So, I need to tell you something," Jamie said. "Do you know a girl named Violet?"

"No."

"Well, her stepfather is Lester Hightower."

"Oh, yeah, I think I've seen her."

"Apparently Brendan was at her house before . . ."

"The crash?"

"Yeah. And she thinks her stepfather had something to do with it."

Sophia's face lit up, and Jamie wanted to holler, or sing, or jump up and down. He told her about Rosa Perez, and right then and there it was decided—they would find out what really happened that night, and hopefully clear themselves of the horrible guilt they'd been carrying around like a backpack full of stones. They immediately got an Uber into town and then boarded the interisland ferry to Martha's Vineyard. On the top deck, Sophia told him about her new school and how it was nice to be anonymous. Jamie told her how he'd spent most of last year working on the student newspaper and hanging out with his elderly neighbor, working on a nonfiction piece about her.

As they waited in line to exit the ferry, Jamie grabbed Sophia's hand and she squeezed. They were in this together.

Vineyard Haven was not exactly postcard pretty. There were trucks and exhaust fumes, and a few run-down motels. They went to the restaurant Violet had told him Rosa worked at. One of the busboys was smoking in the alley next to it, and Sophia turned on her charm. He had never seen her act this way . . . what was the word, sultry? Whatever it was, they got the info. Rosa wasn't there but lived on a catamaran moored off the main docks. When they left she actually blew the busboy a kiss. As they walked toward the docks, Jamie said, "I've never seen you do that."

"You haven't seen nothing yet," she said, and Jamie laughed.

They reached the main marina and stared at the boats that floated in the harbor. There were two catamarans, and one had a Mexican flag on the bow.

"That must be hers," Sophia said.

"Right."

A few minutes later a man puttered in on an old dinghy, not bothering to take the key out of the engine. After he was out of sight, Sophia said, "Okay, we're here, and we have only two hours until the ferry goes back. I know how to drive a dinghy, so let's do it. And if you say one thing I'll change my mind, so shut up."

Jamie felt his pulse quicken. He nodded vigorously, and they got into the dinghy. Five minutes later, they were pulling up to the catamaran with the Mexican flag.

"That boat sleeps six," Sophia said. "She must have boatmates."

They motored around it but didn't see any occupants. "Hello?" Jamie called out.

A hippie guy came out, holding a small drum.

"Hi, sorry to bother you, but we're looking for Rosa," Sophia said. "We met her the other day, and she left something behind."

Again, Jamie couldn't believe his ears. Sophia lying twice in one afternoon?

The hippie smiled from ear to ear.

"Ah, no problem. You want to leave it with me?"

A large motorboat went by, packed with people drinking and laughing. They waited for them to pass, and then Jamie said, "We'd rather give it to her in person, if you don't mind."

"No worries. She's down at the Shipyard Tavern."

"Thanks, Dude." Jamie had never really said "dude" before, but if he was going to say it to anyone, it would be to this guy.

The man smiled again and said, "No worries."

Sophia pulled the dinghy back into the spot where they'd found it, and then they hurried out. When they got onto the dock and started walking, Jamie couldn't stop smiling. He looked over and noticed Sophia was too. They had just borrowed a dinghy and gotten away with it.

Rosa was alone at one end of the bar, nursing a beer. Jamie and Sophia approached her cautiously, sitting down on stools close to her. They ordered french fries and two Cokes. When the fries came, Jamie found himself smiling at Rosa, who seemed weary, a woman who was clearly beautiful but broken down by life. Jamie secretly prayed he and Sophia and Trevor weren't a part of that.

"Excuse me, are you Rosa?" Sophia asked, diving right in.

She looked up, at first with fear in her eyes, but then she smiled realizing that Jamie and Sophia were teenagers.

"You used to know Brendan Daly, right?" Sophia continued.

"Who are you?" she said in a quiet voice with a thick accent.

"Sorry," Jamie said. "This is Sophia, and I'm Jamie. We're researching his accident because we think there may have been more to it."

"Sorry, my English is so-so."

Jamie was immediately grateful for Sophia's two years of Honors Spanish. The two of them started talking, and Jamie knew what was being said went beyond platitudes. The woman immediately warmed up to Sophia, as people usually do when you speak in their native tongue.

Jamie took French but knew a little Spanish, so he could get the gist of what Sophia was saying. Something about "getting to the bottom of it." He felt proud of Sophia's expertise. Rosa started speaking, slowly at first but then really fast. Still, Jamie could tell Sophia was understanding all of it. Rosa finished her beer and then gestured that she had to go. Both Sophia and Jamie thanked her, and they paid their bill and left, making their way back to the ferry terminal. They sat on the sad little beach by the entrance, and Sophia filled Jamie in.

"She called him her 'muñeco,' which means 'doll.' She obviously loved him, a lot."

They watched some little kids chase pigeons on the dock.

"This is what kills me," Jamie said. "Brendan Daly had a life, like everyone else, and is probably missed more than we can even fathom. Did he have kids?"

"No. She said the accident was, well, she used the Spanish word *mystified* but I think she meant *mystery*. She said that Brendan had no family, was raised in Maine in what she called a 'house for children,' which I'm assuming meant an orphanage. When she met him, he'd started working for what she called 'the rich guy' in Nantucket, commuting from the Cape, where they lived together in a room above a garage. She said Brendan loved Lester. It was all he ever talked about. He wanted to be like him one day, which was 'silly' as she put it. Brendan had even bought himself one of those belts with turtles on them— she said turtles, but I think she meant whales."

"Jeez, your Spanish is really good."

"It's nice to be able to use it in real life. Anyway, she said that Brendan and his construction partner ended up investing all of their money with Lester. The day before the accident, Brendan had been on the phone with Lester, and was very angry. He wanted the money back, and she used a word I didn't know but I think meant 'dividends.' Then the next day, he said he was going to Lester's big party. The last thing she asked him was if he was invited, and he said no."

"So there was another party in Sconset that night," Jamie said.

"Yes, at Lester Hightower's."

Jamie's head swam with questions.

"Did she say who Brendan's partner was?"

"She didn't say his name, just called him 'un hombre,' a guy. I asked her what he looked like, and she said 'rojo,' which I guess meant red hair or that he's Irish. She also mentioned that the guy's mother lives on Nantucket, in Madaket."

On the ferry back, they sat on the top deck again, but this time right at the front, like explorers. They didn't speak, instead just took it all in. The crisp sea air, the bow splitting the water into whitecaps, the distant shoreline of Nantucket beckoning.

As the ferry turned into the sound, seagulls guided the boat, like racers running ahead of the pack.

Sophia turned to Jamie and said, "I don't think it was us. I really don't."

Jamie could see her eyes welling up, and he could feel his own doing the same. The horn of the ferry blasted, startling them, and then they started to laugh.

Sophia rested her head on Jamie's shoulder as the boat slowed to dock.

"Well, one thing's for sure," Jamie said. "We're going to find out."

The next morning they rode bikes out to Madaket, a small town on the west end of the island with only one restaurant, a small store, and a long stretch of beach where some families were having picnics. They decided to go to the restaurant, because if anyone was going to know the residents, it would be the waiters. They ordered a quesadilla and iced teas, sat outside on the patio and talked about Sophia's favorite subject—college.

"My essay has only one prompt," Sophia said. "I guess they're all different."

"What does it say?"

"It asks what is unique about me."

"You'll kill it, Soph. You always do."

"I'm not so sure anymore. And don't say 'kill.'"

"Right."

The waitress, a nice older lady who was overly tan and weathered, asked if they needed anything else.

"Well, there is one thing," Jamie said. "I'm looking for a friend of mine that used to live here with his mother, did construction?"

The waitress hardly blinked. "Shamus? Oh, he's long gone. I heard he runs a kiteboarding school in Tulum. His mother still comes in though. She's the house across the bridge there."

How easy was that? Maybe Jamie should blow off journalism and be a private investigator. It seemed that he and Sophia had a knack for it.

"Oh yeah, what's her name again?"

"Her name is Riley. Not a forgettable name for a woman." The waitress smiled and took away their plates.

They paid and then walked over the bridge that connected the street to the dunes where Riley's house was. They knocked on the door, but no one answered. A few minutes later, an old pickup truck pulled into the driveway. The woman driving, who they assumed was Riley, seemed a little taken aback that people were standing on her porch.

"Hi, can I help you?" she asked.

This time Sophia took the lead.

"Yes, we're sorry to just show up like this, but are you Riley?"

"That depends," the woman said with a smirk. "Are you from the IRS?"

Jamie and Sophia looked at each other and smiled as Riley pulled a case of beer out of the back of her truck.

"No, we're just high school kids. We're actually investigating a car accident that happened in Sconset last summer."

The woman froze, then put the beer down on the porch railing.

"Now, why would two nice kids like yourselves get involved in solving crimes?"

"Who said it was a crime?"

The woman looked off into the distance, like she was calculating something in her head. Then she got really serious. "Look, I'm going to need to open one of these to have this conversation," she said. "Come on in."

Jamie and Sophia followed her inside. On her fridge was a picture of a red-haired guy holding a big fish and grinning. It must have been Shamus, Brendan's partner.

Riley told them to sit down. The sun through the windows made elongated lines in the kitchen, which to Jamie resembled a jail cell.

She took a long drink and sighed. "So, you knew Brendan?"

"You could say that," Jamie replied.

"Do you know Shamus? My son?"

"No," Sophia said. "But we've heard of him. He's in Mexico?"

"Yes. What is it you want to know about Brendan? There's nothing to know, really. He was drinking and driving. So sad. I hope you guys don't do that."

"The article mentioned there was alcohol in his system, but

there was something else that may have happened. Did you know the person he worked for?"

"No."

It was clear that she was lying. Jamie could tell by the way she cleared her throat and looked to the left—classic lying behavior. He decided to try a different tactic. If Sophia took the lead with Rosa, he could do the same with Riley.

"So why did Shamus leave?" he asked.

"Came into some money. Always wanted to leave the island."

At the mention of money, Jamie had an idea.

"So, I guess he worked for Hightower as well?"

"You said it, not me," Riley said, taking another extra-large sip of her beer.

If only they could talk to Shamus. Jamie was sure he knew a lot more than Riley did.

"Do you know anything more about Brendan or the accident?"

Riley wiped her mouth with her sleeve, and Jamie could see her eyes tearing up. Clearly they were bringing back dark memories for her.

"Brendan was a good boy. They grew up together, Shamus and him. Thick as thieves. But that's the thing about being parents. The kids become adults. What they got into, well, it was their own choice."

"Was Shamus at the Hightower's the night Brendan died?"

"No. He was DJing another party."

Again, Jamie thought she was holding something back. She didn't clear her throat or look away, but her voice quivered. Then she excused herself.

While Riley was in the bathroom, Jamie noticed an old-school address book, worn at the edges, and felt a magnetic pull to it. His eyes widened as he frantically turned to the "S" section. There it was—Shamus, with an address in Tulum and a number that had ten digits and an (01) in front of it.

"That must be his number in Mexico!" He stage-whispered to Sophia.

He heard the toilet flush as he searched for a pen. He started writing the number on his hand but the pen wasn't working, so he grabbed an old piece of mail instead.

"Jamie!" Sophia whispered back.

He scribbled the digits as fast as he could. The latch on the bathroom door opened, and he shut the book and shoved the envelope in his pocket, just in time.

Riley downed the rest of her beer.

"So what are you saying, exactly?" she asked. "That someone else was involved?"

"Well, there may have been foul play."

She laughed, and Jamie could see her yellow teeth. She opened another beer and kept laughing, but it turned into more of a whine. Was she attempting to cry?

"Brendan, he was a good boy," she repeated. "It really did a number on my Shamus."

"I'll bet. I'm so sorry ... we are so sorry about what happened."

Riley slammed her hand on the counter, and Sophia flinched.

"What do you have to be sorry for?"

Jamie and Sophia looked at each other gravely, then turned back to Riley.

"Nothing," Sophia said after a weighted silence. "We should go. Thanks so much for your time."

She slammed her hand down again.

"So that's it? You're going to come in here and stir up this horrible stuff and leave? What is your connection to Brendan, anyway?"

Neither of them had an answer. Jamie stared at the door, which was still slightly opened. After a heavy pause, Sophia saved the day. "I knew his girlfriend, Rosa."

"Rosa." She took another sip and shook her head. "Another good kid. She still in Vineyard Haven?"

"Yes."

"Well, I don't know what you all are looking for, but this Hightower man, he's a powerful guy. He's got a lot at his disposal. I'd be careful if I were you."

"Thanks, we will," Jamie said.

They walked toward the door, and she said, in a louder voice, "Why don't you just be teenagers for a while, how about that. Like, do teenager stuff."

*That's what got us into this mess*, Jamie thought.

When they got outside, he felt relieved.

"I thought she was going to freak out," he said.

"She kind of did," Sophia said. "I can't believe you risked writing down that number."

Jamie could tell that Sophia was not only surprised but kind of impressed.

As they headed back to their bikes, they brainstormed frenetically, cutting each other off with their questions and ideas. Did Hightower pay the cops off? What did Riley mean by "a lot at his disposal"? Is that why Shamus left, to flee Lester?

As they rode back, Jamie watched Sophia's hair in the wind. In spite of everything, it calmed him. When they got to the Sconset rotary, they stopped before parting ways.

"There's definitely something fishy going on, no pun intended," Sophia said. "You need to talk to Violet more."

"Yeah, but first let's call this number. Can we use your mom's phone?"

"I guess."

When they got to Sophia's house, it was empty.

"They are probably on their walk," Sophia said, "which means we have twelve minutes, tops."

They hurried back into the office and dialed the frantically scribbled numbers only Jamie could read.

A woman who didn't speak English answered the phone, so Jamie immediately gave the phone to Sophia.

Hearing her talk in Spanish, he prayed she was finding out something, or that maybe Shamus would get on the phone. But when she hung up, her face fell.

"Shamus used to live there, but only for a couple weeks. She doesn't know where he is now."

"Ugh."

They could hear Sophia's moms coming back from their walk. As Jamie and Sophia passed them in the kitchen, they both tried to act normal, but Jane and Courtney knew something was up. Jamie could tell they thought it was some teenage thing, like Jamie and Sophia were kissing in the back or something. If only it was something that simple. That was the thing—adults thought they knew everything, but a lot of times they had no idea.

At the end of Sophia's driveway, Jamie got on his bike, but before he could ride away, Sophia put her hand on his arm. "Wait. There's something I need to tell you. I should have told you this a long time ago, but I feel like if we're not completely honest with each other nothing is going to get solved."

Jamie knew by looking at her face that a bomb was about to be dropped. Sophia paused. He could feel a trickle of sweat run from his armpit down his side.

"We hooked up, Trevor and me. Last winter. I wanted to tell you and he didn't, which was the reason we broke up, basically. I'm so sorry, Jamie. None of this was supposed to happen."

Sophia started to cry.

Jamie's face went slack. He was speechless. Trevor and Sophia?

"It was nothing. Jamie . . ."

He felt like he could really break something, which is why his first instinct was to just ride away. If he stayed in her presence, he might explode.

# CHAPTER 7

# VIOLET

The first time she met Lester, he thought she was the help.

A few months had passed since her father had moved to California. Violet was wiping down the counters of their Beacon Hill apartment when her mother had walked in with Lester, clearly after a liquid lunch. Violet wasn't really on speaking terms with her, so it didn't faze her that she didn't introduce Lester, who barely acknowledged Violet anyway. The two of them headed upstairs, giggling. In a way, she was happy for her mother. She was living recklessly, drinking during the day, dating guys, wearing more revealing outfits. Ironically, it was what Violet should've been doing. But Violet never really liked alcohol, and the boys who courted her seemed so immature. She was kind of basic during that time, doing homework and watching reruns of *Grey's Anatomy* on Netflix.

A few minutes later Lester came down to get some water, again barely noticing Violet, who was now getting ready to take out the trash. When he did finally notice her, he made a face, like a great idea had just come to him.

"Do you have a card?"

"What?" Violet said.

"My cleaner just disappeared—I hope she wasn't deported!" He laughed and continued. "Anyway, I need a new cleaner, and thought . . ."

"Seriously?"

Lester started realizing his faux pas, putting his hand over his face.

"Yeah, I'm the daughter. The half Hispanic one. I'd give you my card, but I may get deported soon."

"Oh shit, I'm such a dummy."

*Dummy?* Violet had thought. *More like a racist scumbag.*

"I'm so sorry. You must be Violet."

"Ding! You got it, Einstein."

He laughed, and a gold filling in his mouth flashed. Lester reached out to shake her hand. Firm grip but clammy. She felt nauseous and happy to have the excuse to leave the kitchen, trash now in hand. After loading the bag into the bin on the curb, she sat on the stoop, shaking her head. *What a douche. Where did she find him?*

After she told Kaila, it became a thing. Kaila made Violet a T-shirt that said "I'm not the help." She could wear it in Nantucket, where people often thought she was a nanny. It was embarrassing, but a reality. The island was diverse, but not in some circles, especially the summer people on Baxter Road.

The next time she'd seen Lester, they all went out to dinner. Violet hadn't told her mother about the more than awkward encounter when they'd first met, and Lester was trying extra hard to make up for it, doting on Violet and telling her that she was so pretty—so much so that her mother was getting jealous. Normally Violet would've enjoyed the attention, but coming from Lester it felt creepy. She left the dinner early, claiming Kaila was having a crisis, which she kind of was. Kaila was always in some sort of crisis.

In fact, right now, walking off the ferry, Kaila was in crisis mode. Violet hugged her, so glad her best friend could get away from Boston for a night, even if it was under these circumstances. Kaila's current boyfriend had told her he was seventeen, but she found out he was twenty. Violet didn't think it was that big of a deal, but for Kaila it was the end of the world.

As they drove up island, her best friend started crying. She'd always been emotional, so Violet was used to it. She'd lost her father to a shack in California; having a slightly older boyfriend was hard to drum up empathy for. But she tried, holding Kaila's hand with her free one and squeezing just a little.

"Hey, don't even give him that."

"Vi, I was, I don't know, I was actually seeing a future with him. Now there's no way."

"'Cause he's five years older than you?"

"It just won't work. He told me he was in high school, and he's about to graduate college!"

Violet knew that Kaila had her life mapped out. She was interning this summer with a trendy start-up and already planning her post-college career when she still had a year of high school left.

They stopped for ice cream at Island Kitchen. Violet tried to distract Kaila by telling her about meeting Jamie and how him and his friends think they caused Brendan's accident but that she'd always thought there was something else going on that involved Lester.

"As much as I love the beach house, the boat, having a freaking *butler*, I need to take sketchy Lester down."

"Girl, you watch too much Netflix."

"He did something that night, I know it."

"Vi, Brendan was the one who drove into the tree."

"You should've seen the look on Jamie's face when he thought he might be exonerated or whatever. It was like he'd had a glimpse of heaven."

"Is he our age?" Kaila asked.

"Wait, are you already on the market?"

"Maybe a rebound hookup?"

Violet smiled. She and Kaila had always been safe, but definitely ahead of their peers in that department. She learned about confidence from Kaila, which had changed the whole game. One time, at this stupid dance, Kaila just walked up to this senior quarterback and kissed him. Violet ended up with the tight end.

When they got back to the house, Ricardo welcomed Kaila by kissing her on both cheeks.

"Welcome to the one percent!" Ricardo said, and the three of them laughed. "Lester's in New York, and your mom is, where do you think?"

"Playing tennis," Violet said.

"What can I say, they are predictable. But guess what? I made you girls a picnic lunch you can take down to the beach!"

"Thanks, Rickie. You're the best."

"De nada, Babygirl."

After they changed into their suits, Violet grabbed the retro picnic basket Ricardo had stuffed with fixings, threw Kaila some towels, and they were off through the backyard and down the steps.

"This place is like, so glamorous," Kaila said.

"I know. I just wish it wasn't funded with dirty money."

"Money is money, Girl."

"Not really."

They set up their towels at the bottom of the stairs in the fine white sand, then immediately jumped into the water. It was cold but refreshing. The thing about swimming in the ocean was you could escape from your thoughts. There was so much stimulation; it was all too beautiful and unthinkable. The water seemed to breathe, undulating for miles and miles.

"Let's swim to Spain," she said to Kaila when they both resurfaced.

"You can. I'll take your stepfather's jet and meet you there."

They dove under a wave and came up laughing.

As another big wave approached, Kaila said, "Let's ride it in!"

The wave took the two of them gracefully, but then plopped them down on the sand with a thud. They got up, giggling all the way back to their towels.

As Kaila checked her phone, Violet watched the roiling Atlantic, thinking of her father on the Pacific. Even though all the oceans were connected, she felt so far from him right then.

The lunch was chicken wraps and homemade salsa with chips. Ricardo had also packed chilled Fiji water bottles and little mint chocolate cookies.

"I could get used to this life," Kaila said.

"I know. But I want it for myself, you know?"

"Yeah, me too."

"My mother calls Lester a 'Wheeler and a Dealer.' More like Sketcher and a Schemer."

"Yeah but, you know what they say, don't bite the hand that feeds you."

"What about chopping it off?"

Kaila laughed. An older couple, wearing linen and smiling at each other, walked by with two bumbling Labradors.

"It's like an ad for Viagra," Violet said.

"Stop."

"Or the latest feel good drug that makes you suicidal."

"Yeah, with a name that sounds really hopeful."

"Zoloft."

"Elavil."

"What's your dad on…"

"He was on Cymbalta. And no, it didn't help."

They both looked at their phones for a second, like a reflex.

"He keeps texting me," Kaila said.

"Ugh, next."

"Speaking of, what's up with Chad?"

"I'm kind of over him too. Got other fish to fry."

She didn't, really, but she just knew she'd grown out of Chad. In fact, she changed his name in her contacts to *Do not answer*.

As Kaila fell asleep in the sun, Violet looked up and saw her mother on the stairs, motioning for her. She sighed, then started up to meet her halfway.

"I see she's fitting right in," her mother said, pointing toward Kaila.

"She's kind of been through a lot this week."

"Oh, I'm sure," her mother said patronizingly, like teenager problems were just over-dramatic. In this case she was kind of right, but what about Jamie and his friends? They were dealing with what might have been *murder*. Is that a problem less important than an adult's? She felt a wave of anger toward her mom and tried to stifle it with a deep breath, but it didn't work.

"You wouldn't know anything about it, because you have no problems now. Your only problem moved to California."

Violet immediately regretted saying that, but sometimes her mouth was a broken dam and the rush of words just flowed out and she couldn't stop them. This occasional river of vitriol wasn't her best quality.

"That's not fair," her mother said, moving her sunglasses onto the top of her head. "What's wrong? Did you have a fight with Kaila?"

"No. It's actually Lester. Do you know more about his relationship with Brendan? What happened the night he died?"

"Honey, we've been through this. It was an accident. A terrible accident."

It was true. Violet had tried to bring it up like, ten times, but her mother had blinders on.

"Mom ... seriously, how much do you really know about Lester?" She'd almost called him *Sketcher*.

"What are you talking about?"

Her mother was offended. Violet knew the look; it meant the conversation was over.

"Forget it. I'm gonna go back down. Are you coming?"

"No, I was just checking on you girls. I'm headed to the farmers market. You know Ricardo and his tomato obsession."

She sounded like another person entirely. Getting tomatoes for her butler? Violet remembered being younger, when her parents were happy, even in their small place in Jamaica Plain. They didn't have much, but life seemed easier then—more real.

"We'll always have Jamaica Plain," Violet said.

"What?"

"Nothing." *Just everything*, she thought. "Okay, bye, Mom."

"Have fun!"

Kaila was still asleep, so Violet swam some more, picturing her father doing the same, only three thousand miles away. Why couldn't he be here, right now, with his only daughter? It wasn't fair.

When she got back to the towels, Kaila had just woken up, stretching her arms high. "I feel so much better now. Let's go find dead things!"

So they went searching. The shells of crabs were kind of cute, the carcasses of fish were gross, and the remains of a seagull was downright disgusting, but Kaila loved it. She had always been into dead things.

That night they watched Netflix in the "movie room," eating gourmet popcorn and drinking Diet Cokes. Kaila fell asleep (again!), and Violet found herself wandering over to the corner of the basement where Ricardo lived. She put her ear to the door. He was listening to some schmaltzy song from the *Titanic* soundtrack. Violet knocked.

He opened the door, wearing a silk robe.

"Coming to see how the other half lives?"

Violet smiled. "Can I come in?"

"You know what? I don't think that's appropriate, but I'll come out, okay?"

"Okay."

They went into another room in the basement that housed a pool table and a couple of fancy beanbags. Violet sat on the pool table, and Ricardo took a beanbag.

"Look, I know it was last summer and no one likes to talk about it, but this whole Brendan thing is coming to the forefront again."

"Babygirl . . ."

"I know you are loyal to my mother, but I promise I won't tell her you told me anything. You can trust me. What do you know about that night? As you know, I was in Boston with Kaila so . . ."

"Why are you bothering with this?"

"Because, Ricardo, Brendan was a *person*. And I think that Lester had something to do with all of it."

Ricardo stood up and paced a little, then he stopped and took a deep breath.

"It was a crazy night. I was the only one cleaning up because the caterers had left early. Your mother had gone to bed. I remember that Brendan was in Lester's office for a long time. Before I retired myself, I heard some yelling."

"Who? Lester or Brendan? Who was yelling?"

"Let's just say things were *acalorado*. But you know, I could lose my job if Lester . . ."

"I told you, Ricardo, it's cool. We never had this conversation."

"Okay, but can I give you a little bit of advice? You really don't want to mess with Lester."

"I'm not afraid of him."

Ricardo made a noise and turned back before leaving the room.

"I am," he said.

○ ○ ○

Violet had her recurring dream that night. She was swimming in the sea, except the water was clear, almost white, like in a commercial for some exotic resort. Laser beams of light from a bright yellow sun danced off the water in every direction. Violet kept swimming, faster and faster. There was an island ahead of her, with trees that looked like overgrown broccoli. In spite of how fast she was moving, every time she came up for air the island was in the same place. She wasn't getting closer, and she barely had any strength left.

When she woke up, Kaila wasn't next to her. She tried to collect her thoughts, situate herself. She was in Nantucket, in the house of a potentially very bad man.

Over on the table by the window stood the box of pencils, and on the wall to the side of it, the taped postcards from her father. She picked out a color and threw up her hair, sliding the pencil through a knot. She put on some jeans and a top and headed down the stairs, stopping at the sound of laughter from the kitchen. It was Lester, she could tell from the booming voice. He always laughed a little too hard at his own jokes.

When she got to the door of the kitchen, which was cracked slightly open, she peered in. Lester was pouring Kaila some coffee, smiling ear to ear. When Kaila wasn't looking, he pushed a spoon off the counter, and it clattered on the tile floor.

"Oh, shoot. Could you grab that for me? My back's been flaring up."

"Sure," Kaila said. When she bent over, Lester eye-groped her, having orchestrated the whole thing. Kaila was clueless.

"Gross," Violet said as her mother came up behind her.

"What?" her mother asked.

"Nothing," Violet said, even though when anyone says that it's always something. She wished her mother could read the signs. They were practically neon. But like Kaila, she was oblivious. They both walked into the kitchen, and Lester offered her mother some coffee with cream in it. *Does he not know she drinks it black?* Her mother took it anyway, and Violet shot her a look.

"So," Lester said, "Kaila was telling me about her internship in Boston. Pretty impressive. Maybe some of that ambition will rub off on you, Violet."

Her mother raised her eyebrows, as if agreeing that was a good idea. Was it just Violet's imagination, or were all three of them ganging up on her now?

"Whatever," Violet said, grabbing a yogurt from the fridge. "I'm going out back. You coming?" she asked Kaila, but didn't wait for her to answer.

Outside, the sun's morning rays were already stretching across the lawn as the ocean lapped the shore down below. It was beautiful here, there was no denying that. But sometimes underneath beautiful things lurked darkness, even poison. Violet had always been tuned into vibes and stuff, ever since she was a child. Meeting Jamie, and being reminded of Brendan, maybe it was all a sign. Sometimes those seeds of darkness needed to be unearthed. And Lester would have to pay if he had a part in Brendan's death. How's that for ambition?

They spent the morning on the beach. Kaila was preoccupied by her phone. Violet figured that once it sunk in, she was going to forgive her boyfriend.

"Do you like him? Sketcher?" Violet wanted to know.

"What do you mean?"

"You were laughing with him."

"Well, he's a little goofy, but I think he's harmless."

*How nice it would be*, Violet thought, *to be so wrapped up in your own world that you can't even see that Lester is more than goofy.*

"I think he's dangerous," Violet said.

Kaila laughed, but it sounded fake.

"Just be aware," she added.

"You really are creeped out by him, huh?"

"Well, yeah, I am."

During the ride into town later, Violet and Kaila didn't talk much. They didn't need to. The truth was, Lester was right— Kaila had more ambition than her. She always had. But Violet knew it wasn't something you could gain overnight. She needed passion, and a purpose. She had a taste of that with sailing and teaching the Boys & Girls Club kids. But what she was feeling about Lester was larger than that. It could affect her and her mother's future. Jamie and his friends as well.

At the ferry terminal, they hugged awkwardly in the car.

"Keep me posted, and be careful," Kaila said, like she could hear Violet's thoughts.

On her way home, Violet stopped by the luncheon benefit at the Yacht Club to see if any of her kids were there, the ones she took sailing when she volunteered. The only kid she recognized was Madeline, a redheaded girl who smiled at her and hugged her leg. Most of the guests were drinking wine and mingling. When Violet grabbed a mini crab cake off a waiter's tray, she met his eyes: Jamie.

"Hey," he said.

"Hi," Violet said, eating the crab cake in one bite. "What's going on?"

"Working," Jamie said.

"I can see that."

"Oh, and I found out my friends Trevor and Sophia had contact over the school year. Like, physical contact."

"Ouch."

"The whole thing basically sucks. What's up with you?"

"Well, I got something out of Ricardo. Not much, but he told me Brendan was in Lester's office for a long time before he left that night, and they were arguing."

Jamie looked around the party anxiously.

"You have to go, I know," Violet said.

"Hey, do you have security cameras in your house?"

Violet pictured the little glass orbs throughout the property. "Definitely on the exterior, but good idea. I'll check."

"Okay, text me later."

Jamie was off with his tray of crab cakes, and Violet snuck out of the event as quick as she had come in. Driving up Milestone Road, past the fields dotted with scrub oaks, she kept thinking about what Jamie said. *Security cameras.* That would shed light on a lot of things. If she could just *see* it instead of *feel* it . . . bring the truth to light.

She drove a little faster.

On Baxter Road, she saw a girl walking a chocolate lab. Blond ringlets. Super cute. Wearing a Brown sweatshirt and cutoff jeans. The girl waved at Violet, who waved back. It wasn't until she pulled into her driveway that she realized who it must have been: Sophia. Jamie had told her she always wore Brown swag. Violet didn't understand her hooking up with Trevor, a.k.a. Pretty Boy, but who was she to judge? Her so-called boyfriend was a flaky video game addict.

There was no one inside the house, which always freaked her out because it was so big. Lester and her mother were probably playing golf, and Ricardo was most likely down in Tom Nevers park, where a lot of the Hispanic workers on the island played soccer and hung out on Sundays, drinking beers and laughing, playing music out the backs of their cars. She went one Sunday, but she always felt inauthentic, being only half Hispanic and not completely fluent in Spanish.

She immediately went into Lester's office, where some music was coming out of a Bluetooth speaker. It sounded like elevator music, which always made Violet anxious. Why was the music on? She looked around the periphery of the ceiling. No cameras. There was, however, a conspicuous owl she'd never seen before on one of the bookshelves. She picked it up, expecting to see a camera inside it, when she heard a voice in her ear.

"Can I help you with something?"

She dropped the owl, and one of its eyes popped off, rolling in between her feet. It was Lester, who had seemed to appear out of nowhere.

"What the . . ."

"Violet. What are you doing in here?"

She told herself to chill and not be afraid, or at least not show it. But Lester was breathing through his mouth, like he was some kind of hungry predator ready to eat Violet whole.

"I had never seen that owl before, I was just . . ."

"Snooping? Look, Violet, I'm an open book." He held out his arms. Did he want her to hug him? Fat chance.

"I know, I mean . . ."

"What do you want to know?" he asked.

Then it happened. Her mouth, the broken dam. The words like a river.

"What was going on with you and Brendan's business deal?"

Lester had a smile that looked stapled to his face.

"He was a worker, that's all."

"Everyone knew he was investing with you. What did you do? Lose all his money?"

"Wow, the third degree from my stepdaughter."

"Why don't you wipe that stupid smile off of your face and just tell me," Violet said, forming her hands into fists at her sides.

Something switched and his face went dark. He grabbed her by the shoulders and squeezed hard.

"That's none of your business, little girl, is it?"

"I'm not a little girl," Violet said, but it came out like a whimper.

He stared at her, seething, like he might slap her.

Violet picked up the owl and put it back on the shelf, then retrieved the loose eye and dropped it into his palm.

"Thanks," Lester said, relaxing, like everything was normal. "I'll have Ricardo reattach this. We can't have a one-eyed owl, can we?" He laughed, a little too loud, and Violet knew, right then, that she was right. Lester wasn't telling her the truth. He had something to hide.

● ● ●

That night she played her ukulele and spoke to Alida, the nice woman who lived near her father, who gave her an update. He was the same. Surfing a little in the mornings and reading in his shack in the afternoon.

"Can you take him out, maybe? Like to the fish taco place?"

"I will, my dear. Don't worry. He'll get through this."

Violet prayed she was right.

After she hung up, a text came in from Jamie:

*Just finished my shift. Any cameras?*

Violet responded right away.

*No, just an owl.*

*What?*

*Nothing, he kind of caught me in there. And I know he's guilty of something—I just need to figure out what.*

*Yeah.*

*Btw, I saw your friend Sophia. Brown sweatshirt? Brown dog?*

*Yes and yes.*

*Can I give you some advice?*

*Sure*

*Forgive them. I know it's hard. But trust me, you need them.*

*We'll see*

She thought about him trying to kiss her. Should she have let him? Definitely not. Jamie had a lot on his plate. Plus, she wasn't so sure what team he played on. Violet texted him again:

*Why don't you try to not think about it and get some rest?*

*I will. My aunt just made chili and I'm in a food coma anyway ☺ talk tomorrow*

*k*

Violet tried to do the same. She needed to clear her mind and get some rest, but she kept thinking of her oblivious mother, sleeping in the same bed with that . . . monster. She could still feel his grip on her shoulders. Violet wasn't particularly fond of her mother these days, but the truth was her mother was the only family she had here. Violet needed her. She had to help her.

When she finally did go to sleep, the dream came back. The white ocean, the broccoli-tree island. This time, though, the island *was* getting closer. But when she arrived, she stepped onto the beach and started to sink. It was quicksand. She grabbed at some branches, anything that would keep her above ground, but she was dropping fast—deeper and deeper into the cold, wet sand, until everything turned black.

# CHAPTER 8

# TREVOR

The day he first met Sophia and Jamie was still so clear in his mind, he could almost remember each moment. The three of them were waiting in the parking lot of the movie theater in their town. Jamie was carrying a notebook, and Sophia's blonde hair was pulled back in a tight bun. This tween kid came riding by on his bike and completely wiped out in front of them. His front wheel spun and he flew over the front handlebars. There was an audible thud when he landed. His head was okay, but his arms were covered in blood. You could tell the kid was freaked out, kind of moaning under his breath. Sophia told us to wait with him, and then ran inside to get napkins.

"There's a slick part of the pavement right there," Jamie said. "I think you were going a little too fast on your turn."

Trevor liked Jamie's MO, rationalizing and analyzing the situation so that it didn't seem as scary. It made the kid calm down a little.

"Seven out of eight people in the Netherlands own a bicycle," Jamie said. "If you think about it, one parking space can hold up to twenty bikes, so . . ."

Trevor tuned Jamie out, and so did the kid a little, but Jamie was doing a great job of defusing the situation. Sophia came back with a first aid kit and started going to work. Trevor and

Jamie watched her in awe. She completely took over, cleaning and wrapping the kid's wounds with total precision.

"What's your name?" Trevor asked.

"Arrow."

"What?"

"My parents are weird."

The three of them all laughed and looked at each other. Thinking back, that was the moment that bonded them together, like some kind of magic. They exchanged numbers and started texting and then hanging out, mostly at Trevor's house because it was big and basically unsupervised. Early on, Sophia asked Trevor where his parents were, and he felt exposed. He knew that Sophia and Jamie had normal parents, he could just tell. They were both super well adjusted. Trevor's parents were a different story. He said they worked a lot, which was true, but he didn't get into any other details. Still, he knew his new friends could sense something was up with his parents. Instead of delving into it or challenging each other, they just moved on, like their friendship was some kind of river. They just rode its course, wherever it led. Trevor thought it might lead to him and Sophia hooking up. She had light in her eyes, and an effortless beauty, like she should be running through a field. But Jamie was the buffer. It seemed like they only worked as a threesome—and not that kind of threesome—so Trevor had placed the thought aside.

Until four months after the accident, when Trevor ran into Sophia at a party. What was the party for? Some kid's older brother getting into college? Didn't matter. What mattered was he was standing in front of Sophia, completely unprepared. He'd just smoked some weed with his friend Jasper. Standing in the tiny hallway between the kitchen and the powder room, Sophia looked like some kind of broken cherub. He was broken too, and seeing her made him want to melt into the atmosphere and disappear.

"Hey," Trevor said. He felt a tremor in his core, something happening beyond his control.

"Hi." She looked drowsy. Had she been drinking?

A couple of giggling gay dudes passed by and bumped Trevor closer to her, and he never even made the decision—it seemed inevitable. He just kissed her, and surprisingly, she kissed him back.

Someone told them to get a room, and that's exactly what they did. Trevor led Sophia through the kitchen and up the stairs to a small den with a couch. They made out feverishly, like they were the last two people on earth. Trevor knew it was messed up, that they both were trying to fill some hole. That the real problem was that someone had died on Baxter Road.

After several minutes, Sophia abruptly stood up and said, "I gotta go."

Trevor sighed, leaning back on the couch, completely bewildered.

Two days later she texted him, saying her mothers weren't home and could he stop by?

He did, and they didn't talk about anything, just started making out again right when he walked in the door, as if there was a magnetic force between them. She tasted a little like peanut butter, and Trevor remembered thinking that was weird. Still, they went all the way, right on Sophia's twin bed.

After, they just lay there breathing. He couldn't remember how much time passed before Sophia spoke.

"We can't tell Jamie this," she said.

"What is *this*?" Trevor asked.

"Nothing. I don't know."

"Me neither."

They didn't cuddle. It was strange, like this animalistic thing they had to get out of their systems. Trevor didn't feel the same way as he did when he slept with other girls. He didn't feel that giddy sense of masculine accomplishment. He just felt shame . . . and guilt.

They saw each other only once after that. He took her to a Broadway play. She was fidgety. They barely talked. The magnetic force was malfunctioning.

Now, driving past her cottage on the way to babysit Bryce, he wondered if she still thought of him or that time in her twin bed. Were they just using each other? Would she ever consider him boyfriend material? Obviously not. There was no going back. They'd screwed up. All of them. But Trevor couldn't help but feel it was more his fault than Sophia's and Jamie's. Probably because it was.

He opened the window and let the crisp air at his face. On Milestone Road, the fields on either side stretched for miles, lit by a bright sun from a perfect blue sky. He loved this island, but now it was symbolic of something indelible, like a scar. How could it ever heal?

Today he was taking Bryce to Nobadeer Beach. He told Alison he'd make sure Bryce was looked after the whole time.

In the Jeep on the way there, Bryce seemed excited.

"I usually go to Children's Beach," Bryce said, "which is for like, three-year-olds. This is awesome."

"Yeah, but remember, you can't go into the water without me," Trevor said.

"I can swim, you know."

"I know, but sometimes the waves are big at this beach."

"Bring it," Bryce said, clearly having heard that expression somewhere before.

Trevor couldn't believe the amount of stuff Alison had packed for Bryce: two towels, a blanket, tons of food, juice boxes, beach toys, an iPad, and a giant water bottle. He felt like a father, lugging all the stuff while Bryce ran ahead of him. He tried to remember if his father ever took him to the beach, but all he could recall was Bea, his sweet and kind nanny who basically raised him. She moved back to Uganda when Trevor turned twelve. He wondered what she was doing right now.

They walked past some families to a stretch of the beach that was basically private. After they set up camp, Bryce said, "Can we go in?"

Other than coming down from his espresso high, Trevor felt pretty good. He was starting to like the little guy. Plus, everything was better at the beach. Sun, sand, sky, waves, and yeah, girls in bikinis.

"Okay," Trevor said, "but stick with me."

They played in the shallow part of the surf for a while, then lay down and made sand angels. Trevor found himself closing his eyes for a moment, letting the sun warm his skin and the waves ripple under him. He looked up and saw Bryce right next to him. He did it again, like a micro-nap, but then he looked up and Bryce was gone. How long was the time period in between? It was like thirty seconds. Was that all it took?

He stood up quickly and felt dizzy, then he saw it with laser eyes—Bryce's little head beyond the break in the waves. He looked so little, so insignificant, like a bobbing buoy that could just disappear. Trevor immediately knew something was terribly wrong. He ran full force toward the ocean, diving under the break line, praying he would see Bryce when he came up for air.

When he did, Bryce was there, but the normal look on his face was gone, replaced by one that said, *What the hell am I doing here? I am too young to be swimming in this surf.*

He was right. The kid was getting pulled out by a riptide. Trevor could feel his own breath shorten. "Oh my god," he said under his breath. He told himself, *Don't worry, you have dealt with this before, many times.* But Bryce's face seemed to get more red and terrified—not the kind of fear from seeing a scary movie, the kind of terror of *I might die now.*

"Hang on, Buddy!" Trevor yelled, but his voice caught in his throat. He needed to calm down if this was going to work. But when the water level between them rose and he couldn't see the little man, he started to say, "No, please," begging to some unknown force of nature.

But like Sophia in the parking lot, his instinct kicked in and he knew what to do. He finally closed in on Bryce and said, "Hey, buddy, just stay calm and take my hand. We have to give it a minute, let the tide take us, okay? Don't worry. I'm right here with you."

He was happy to have the kid's hand. He wouldn't let anything happen to him. He couldn't. Not after what had happened last summer.

"I got you," he said, and Bryce whimpered a little, his eyes welling with tears. "Just think of something good, like pizza," Trevor said, "or ice cream."

Bryce said, "What about my neighbor's dog?"

"That works. Yeah, the dog. Hold on. Don't worry."

Eventually, the tide took them sideways and they started moving toward the shore.

"See, Buddy, we just let the ocean do the work," Trevor said.

When they got to the sand, Bryce tried to act like it was no big deal, but he was breathing heavily and definitely in a state of shock.

"Come here, Buddy."

Trevor picked Bryce up and carried him back to their towels, where they caught their breath. Bryce downed some water and started in on his snacks. A few minutes later, the kid seemed to miraculously forget he'd almost drowned. Even though Trevor knew he screwed up and wouldn't ever let that happen again, he felt useful and proud for the first time in a long time. It was a good feeling.

On the way back to town, Bryce was quiet. But when they pulled up to Alison's cottage, he tapped Trevor on the shoulder.

"From now on," Bryce said softly, "when we are going through something hard, we can just remember the riptide. That way we know we'll get through it."

Trevor wiped at his eyes. He couldn't believe this kid.

"That's right, Bryce. You're absolutely right."

● ● ●

Jamie texted Trevor to meet him at the boat graveyard in mid-island, a place they used to hang out last summer. At the end of a long driveway off of Hooper Farm Road loomed these huge sliding wooden doors with a padlock, which was silly, because you could just hop over the stone wall on either side. Today though, the doors were open. Trevor parked in the dirt lot outside the doors and walked through the threshold. He didn't remember the place being such a cool sight—all these once beautiful and perfect boats sitting on stilts and on the ground, in various states of disrepair. An old guy was sanding the bottom of a yacht toward the far end, and a frizzy-haired woman was cleaning the bow of a vintage wooden motorboat.

Jamie was sitting on a stone slab next to an old dinghy that had grass growing through its bottom. The boat had been eaten away by time and looked sad, but Trevor felt lifted, even happy. Maybe it was due to the riptide experience at Nobadeer. He noticed the grass was healthy and tall, fighting back, a symbol of hope.

Unfortunately though, whatever high he was riding was immediately deflated at the sight of Jamie's face. He was looking at Trevor with such derision and disdain, Trevor had to look away.

"What's going on?"

"You tell me, Trevor. Why don't you fill me in . . . or do you want to just keep me in the dark?" Jamie seemed to spit the words out.

What the hell? Jamestown was always pretty passive, non-confrontational. Right then he looked like he might breathe fire or grow horns. Did Sophia tell him? Of course she did.

"She told you."

Jamie didn't confirm, but he didn't have to. The look on his face was worse than anger—he was betrayed.

"It was nothing. We ran into each other, and it just happened."

"Trevor, you just do stuff without thinking about how you're affecting other people. You always have."

"Not . . . not anymore."

"Yeah, right. I can't believe how much Sophia and I worshipped you. For what? You're a joke, Trevor."

"Jamestown, it wasn't just me."

"It was always you! Everything."

"Dude, we were protecting you."

"Oh, yeah. Always thinking of me first, huh?"

"Would you rather we gave you all the details?"

"I don't know, Trevor. I don't know about anything anymore!"

Jamie stormed off toward the exit, but Trevor ran to catch up with him.

"Let me give you a ride . . ."

"I don't need your charity anymore, Trevor."

"Look, we need each other."

"That's what everyone says, but I'm not so sure."

Trevor tried to put his hand on Jamie's shoulder, but he swatted it away.

"Jamestown . . ."

"Don't call me that! Just leave me alone."

Trevor stopped and let his friend continue down the driveway on foot. It wasn't that bad, was it? Did Jamie have a thing for Sophia, was that it? Trevor kicked the dirt below him and then got back into his Jeep.

❂ ❂ ❂

When he got home, his mother asked him to take a ceramic whale dish to the Hightower's, one that she'd been meaning to return. Trevor was glad for something to do. One of his teachers used to say when you *think* too much, it's time to *do*.

At the Hightower's place, the house manager, Ricardo, greeted him and led him into the kitchen, where the stepdaughter, Violet, was eating yogurt. Trevor still found her hot—that sleek black hair and her big brown bedroom eyes—but tried to act cool. He was used to girls just coming to him, doing all the work. Now it was a different story. Had he lost his mojo?

Ricardo put the dish away and left them alone. Trevor was about to leave when Violet threw the yogurt away and opened a cupboard above the fridge, producing a fifth of Jack Daniel's.

"This was in a gift bag my mother brought home. Since they only drink fancy whiskey, they won't miss it. Wanna share it?"

"Uh, yeah," Trevor said. This was completely unexpected. Violet didn't even like him, and he'd never seen her drink. She had a pencil in her hair, as usual, and was wearing a flowing pale-blue dress.

She led him out to the backyard and through the little gate to the stairs that led down to the beach, and they sat on the bench halfway down. She sipped right from the bottle and passed it to Trevor, who did the same. The liquid burned his throat and made him shiver. He didn't care. He liked it. It meant he was going somewhere—a better place than his current world. He needed to blank out Jamie's wounded face, spewing out his words like venom.

Seagulls swerved over the lapping shore. Besides a few fishing boats that were blurry dots in the distance, the sea shimmered all around them. Trevor was used to seeing it, but that day it felt more real somehow.

"I thought you didn't like me," Trevor said as they passed the bottle again.

"I just thought you were a screwup," Violet said. "I don't usually drink, by the way."

"I know. What gives?"

"I'm bored. My father moved to California, off the grid, my mother is clueless, and my stepfather could be dangerous. So, yeah. Day drinking Jack Daniel's seemed like a plan. Especially when I saw you standing in my kitchen."

"Gotcha."

"So, you gonna tell me what happened with Sophia?"

"Wait, how do you even know about that?"

"I'm friends with Jamie."

"Yeah, he just cussed me out about it."

"As he should."

"I guess."

They each took another swig. Trevor felt the liquid warm his blood. Mixed with the late afternoon sun, it made him dizzy for a second.

"You have to be careful with Jamie," she said. "He's the sensitive type."

"You think I don't know that?"

"I think you have your head up your ass."

Trevor laughed. He liked a girl with candor, who wasn't afraid to swear.

"So what's this about Lester being dangerous?"

"Well, you know about the accident, right?"

"Uh, what accident?"

Violet looked at him, as if to say, *Cut the act.*

"Brendan."

"Oh. Yeah . . ."

"He came from here that night. He'd had a fight with Lester. I think Lester might have had a hand in what happened."

Trevor felt everything right then, in a rush. The whiskey, Violet's beautiful almond eyes, the ocean, the sky—and most importantly, a light at the end of a tunnel.

"Shit," was all he could say.

"Brendan worked for Lester. They had some scheme going. Before he left that night, he was in Lester's office for a long time."

Trevor liked what he was hearing. If Violet was right, all three of them could be off the hook.

"What are you going to do?"

"I'm still working on it."

Something told him to kiss her. He leaned in, and they stared at each other, lips an inch apart. Just when it seemed inevitable, she laughed.

"Nice try, Pretty Boy," she said, taking another swig.

"Rain check?" Trevor asked.

"Unlikely," she said.

"You have a boyfriend?"

"Not as of this morning. I dumped him over text."

"Wow. Harsh."

"He was a waste of space. Cute, but not much brains."

"Well, you run a tight ship," Trevor said.

"What's that supposed to mean?"

"I don't know!"

They both laughed, and Violet hid the almost empty bottle under the bench.

"Well, I'm going to my room to play my shitty songs on my ukulele."

"Care if I join?"

"Sure, but no funny stuff."

They laughed again, but this time it was more like elevated giggling.

Trevor had been to the Hightower's a bunch of times, but he didn't recall it being so opulent. Every surface was gleaming—marble, tile, glass, chestnut. Her room was more understated, with just a four-poster bed and a desk by the window, where a massive box of pencils sat, presumably the ones she used to put up her hair. Postcards were taped to the wall. Without looking closer, Trevor knew they were from her father. At least he wrote to her. At least he cared.

She sat on the edge of the bed and strummed the little guitar thing. Trevor sat on the chair by the desk, looking at the giant cotton ball clouds out the window. She sang some lyrics, but Trevor heard only the melody. It was nice. During the second song, he lay down on her plush carpeted floor. At some point he fell asleep, and so did she. They both woke up to the sound of her mother knocking at the door, calling her to dinner.

"Violet? Oh, I see you have a guest. Trevor, right? Why don't you stay for dinner? Ricardo can add another place setting."

Trevor was groggy but definitely hungry, and he knew he wouldn't be missed at home. "Sure," he said.

"Do I have a say in this?" Violet asked, stretching her arms above her head.

"It's cool," Trevor said. "I can take off."

"Well, you two figure it out. Dinner will be served in ten."

Her mother left, and Trevor looked at Violet. They both smiled. He would stay for dinner.

● ● ●

The food was incredible. Trevor had a fridge full of anything he wanted, but no one really cooked, except for the rare days when his mother did. The chicken for the fajitas was perfectly moist. Still, it was weird, because Trevor barely knew these people. Violet's mom wore a tight expression, sipping what looked like chardonnay. He longed for the day where he could just drink in front of people at dinner and it would be acceptable. The thing was, neither of the two adults at the table seemed to be enjoying themselves.

Lester looked constipated or anxious, or both. He cleared his throat loudly and said, "So, how's your old man?"

"Fine, I guess," Trevor said. *Probably cheating on my mother*, he didn't add.

"Tell him to call me. I seem to be sweating dividends these days."

"Gross," Violet said. She was eating only the green peppers.

Ricardo looked cool, like he could star in a movie or something. Trevor made a point to compliment his cooking as he came around to fill their water glasses, like they were at a restaurant. It was a glaring class distinction, but Trevor always thought of himself as an equal, even though he wasn't. He was closer to Electra than his own mother.

"What are your plans for the summer?" Violet's mother asked him.

"I'm taking care of this kid, Bryce. And yeah, surfing."

"Big plans," Violet said.

"What about you, honey?" She looked at her daughter with unveiled skepticism.

"I'm thinking about becoming a detective," Violet said.

Trevor saw Lester squint his eyes a little at her before taking a sip of his scotch.

"Investigating what?" he wanted to know.

"You know," Violet replied, "what people usually investigate. Crimes."

Lester let out a condescending laugh, then took a bite of chicken. Not only was he eating with his fingers, he was chewing like a horse. Trevor never understood how some rich, powerful people acted like animals and got away with it.

Ricardo, who was standing by, added his own two cents. "She is getting very good at her songwriting," he said, clearly trying to veer the subject.

Violet blushed a little, which Trevor loved. It was like a small window opened briefly, and he could see a different side of her. Same as when she talked about her father earlier, on the stairs.

"Yeah, your voice is very soothing," Trevor said. Soothing? He'd never used that word before. He felt like he was out of body, watching himself as a different person. Was it because of what Violet had told him? That this douchebag was at fault, not him?

"So, you're going to be a pop star? Most of them become drug addicts," Lester said.

"Les, don't be negative," Violet's mother said, taking a large sip of her wine.

"Okay, okay. Be a pop star. Just don't be a drug addict."

It was such thoughtless advice. Lester obviously didn't give two shits about Violet. Which made Trevor want to help her.

"My mother is friends with Meghan Trainor's mother," Trevor said. "Maybe I can get you a meeting or whatever."

Violet's eyes widened for a second, but then she laughed it off. "I don't think I'm ready for that."

"You're raw. People respond to that."

Again, Trevor felt like he was watching himself from the outside. Maybe because he'd been so consumed by his own misery, saving Bryce and possibly helping Violet made him feel more human. He smiled at Violet, and she smiled back. This was becoming a pattern.

When the meal was over, Ricardo started clearing the plates. Trevor tried to clear his own, but Lester stopped him.

"Let the man work. What do you think I'm paying him for? Unless you want to get on my payroll." He laughed too loud. Everyone else at the table was clearly disgusted by his remarks. So much so that when Lester left the room, they all sighed. It seemed more likely, now that he'd spent time with him, that Violet was right about Lester.

After dinner, Trevor thanked Ricardo again, and Violet walked him out.

"Be in touch?"

"Yeah," Violet said. "Let's hope he doesn't murder me in my sleep."

"Ha. Well, you have my number now. Text me whenever."

"Okay, Pretty Boy."

"You're the pretty one," he said, squeezing her shoulder before heading out the door.

# CHAPTER 9

# SOPHIA

She had never imagined what it would be like to kiss Trevor, but when she did, it felt like the only thing to do at that moment. The party at Matty G's house was totally boring, so she impulsively did three Jell-O shots, which at least made swallowing the alcohol easier. Trevor was hot, there was no denying it, but it also kind of felt like kissing her brother (if she had one). She didn't remember how they got upstairs to the den and were suddenly half naked on the little couch. Did he carry her? Did he help get her bra open? Who cared. She felt free. It was amazing—until it wasn't. She remembered she was having her period, and that her mothers were friends with Matty G's parents, and she couldn't risk getting caught. She bailed, leaving Trevor flustered and blue-balled.

She waited for him to text her the next day. The day after too. Finally, she texted him after her mothers left to attend some gala in the city. He responded right away. When he got there, they didn't talk, just started kissing. They each took their clothes off hastily, and did it on her bed. It was better than with Elvis, or Braden, or Alexa. They *knew* each other. There was more than just a physical connection—there was emotion. Sophia thought it was scary but also intense, like riding a roller coaster. She may have cried a little, just from feeling so alive after being numb most of the year. He took his time, and was gentle. Afterward, she felt light-headed, but that feeling was soon replaced by an intense wave of guilt. *Jamie*, she thought. *What would Jamie think?*

The next time she saw Trevor, he got them an Uber into the city and tickets to a Broadway show. It was about street kids in New York trying to realize their dreams, and though it was top-notch, Sophia could barely concentrate on it. She kept thinking about Jamie. During the finale, Trevor tried to hold her hand but she pulled it away. On the Uber ride back to Greenwich, she couldn't take it anymore; her boiling point had been reached, so she just started in.

"We have to tell him," she said.

"Sophia, we've been through this."

"It's just not right."

"Stop."

"You stop! You think we can just go on like this? Like what we did is just gonna go away? Get out of your bubble, Trevor."

"Ugh. Can we just sleep on it? Please?"

"Fine."

When she got dropped off, she didn't kiss Trevor goodbye. In fact, she knew she wouldn't kiss him ever again. Her mothers smiled at her, but she walked right by them. She took a long shower and looked at herself in the mirror. She wasn't a girl. She was a young woman, who had done a really stupid thing.

Jane and Courtney were on their cliff walk, a ritual they undertook every day like clockwork when on the island. Bailey scratched at the door to Sophia's room, so she let the dog in. He seemed to look at her with trepidation in his eyes, like he knew Sophia was facing some kind of conundrum. Bailey jumped up on the bed, and Sophia took in his warm, nutty smell. He curled up beside her as she scrolled through her phone. Twitter was a temporary haven she could always become engulfed in. Most of it was depressing, but she became engrossed in a thread about a guy who lost sight in one of his eyes, and instead of complaining and worrying about it, he turned it around and it ultimately made him a more positive person. A text that came in from Jamie immediately drew her back to reality.

*Rosa is on island and has something for us.*

*What? Okay, give me twenty.*

Sophia made the executive decision to use the Uber account Courtney had set up for her, and left them a note explaining she'd "gone to town." When the driver pulled up to Jamie's, he was already waiting outside.

"So, you're not mad at me?" she asked as Jamie got into the car.

The driver turned up the radio a little.

"No," he said. "But what did you see in him? Really?"

"It was just something we had to get out of our systems."

"You mean, you always . . ."

"No! We were just vulnerable. We're not together. We'll never be."

"Never say never."

"Whatever. So what does Rosa have, and when did you get her number?"

"When you went to the bathroom, in the bar in Vineyard Haven. I could tell she was holding something back, so I thought maybe there'd be a chance she'd reach out. Anyway, she came here to get a bike from her cousin or something."

When they got out of the Uber in the Surfside Beach parking lot, Rosa was right there, seated at a picnic table by the food truck. She was looking around like someone might be watching her. She seemed way more nervous here than back in Martha's Vineyard. Was she afraid of Lester?

Rosa pulled an old journal out of her bag that had a car racing stripe on it. The journal looked like it had lived through several natural disasters.

She said some words in Spanish to Sophia, who nodded. Then she was gone.

"She had to go back to the ferry," Sophia explained. "She said she's not sure if it will help us, but she wanted us to have it. We should look through it. But first, let's get some food. I'm starving."

Sophia got them two burgers and iced teas, and as they sat and ate, they started going through the journal. A lot of the entries were unreadable, but there was one page, dated May 2 of last year, that was written with a thick black Sharpie: JREXX.

"That looks like a stock symbol," Sophie said, "I know 'cause of my mom."

She showed him, and they both started googling it like crazy on their phones. It was the symbol for a real estate development company. Apparently the company was involved in an insider trading scandal, and it went public two weeks after Brendan's journal entry.

"This whole thing just got more shady," Sophia said.

"I know. Do you think Lester had Brendan invest and then, I don't know, blackmailed him or something?"

"The question is, if Lester did have something to do with Brendan's death—like your friend Violet is saying—do we really want anything to do with him? I mean, it's not like we're implicated. Something would've happened to us by now."

"Yeah, but don't you want it to go away? The guilt, I mean."

"Yes, I do, but I also think we need to be careful or this guy might try to off us too."

Sophia couldn't eat the rest of her burger. Jamie was ferociously texting Violet, she assumed. Even though she was trying to be cautious, part of her knew it was too late. They were in it now.

○ ○ ○

Back in Sconset, Sophia and Jamie took Bailey on a walk to the lighthouse. Women in tennis whites rode by on bicycles, and landscapers on ladders trimmed the privets that enveloped the houses. Jamie looked like he wanted to say something but couldn't figure out the words. Sophia knew him well enough that she could almost read his brain patterns, even after not having seen him for many months. She really had missed him.

"So," Jamie started, "there's this guy I work with—Cameron."

"Okay . . ."

"He's in college, going into his sophomore year."

"Yeah . . ."

"And he tried to kiss me."

"Wow," Sophia said, without much gusto. It wasn't surprising. Jamie was more pretty than handsome, and he was also more sensitive than most guys. In fact, she wondered why this hadn't happened a long time ago. "Did you kiss him back?"

"No. I kind of freaked out."

"Well, I kissed a girl that lives on my block back in Connecticut—Alexa."

"What?"

"I'm not gay, but I liked it."

"That's not really like you."

"Well, things change, Jamie."

It was a dumb answer, but she didn't want to go into it. The accident had made her feel dazed and disconnected, and she'd been doing whatever she could to eradicate the emptiness.

"Yeah. So after the Cameron debacle . . . I tried to kiss Violet, and that backfired, so it's all been kind of an epic fail. But I've been texting Cameron a lot, and I think I might try and kiss him, like, when I'm actually prepared, just to see. Did you know giraffes are more homosexual than hetero?"

Sophia laughed. Jamie still had his endless weird fact obsession. She had a vision of them, old, on a front porch somewhere, with Jamie still coming up with random facts. The thought warmed her.

"Well, that solves everything."

"King penguins are mostly gay too."

"Of course they are. All the cool animals."

Bailey raised his big head and barked a little, as if to say *what about dogs?* She loved Bailey more than any human being, that was for sure, but he was definitely hetero.

"The thing is, why should we have to choose? There are scientists that say being bisexual, or fluid as some people say, is the most natural state of being for humans."

"That's farfetched, but you should definitely kiss him. What do you have to lose?"

"Well, people still judge, I guess."

"Anyone who judges, you don't want to be around them anyway."

"True."

When they got to the lighthouse, Sophia let Bailey free from his leash. He started galloping around the tall grass in a state of pure dog bliss.

"Stay away from the cliff!" she yelled, and Bailey looked back. The dog could tell from Sophia's tone that she meant be careful.

Some tourists on rental bikes pulled up and got off, taking pictures in front of the lighthouse. As lighthouses go, it was remarkable. It looked like it belonged in a museum. Tall and white with a bold red stripe and a rotating light . . . what was the word? Majestic.

Bailey came over to check in, slobbering a little on Sophia's jeans, then started running around again.

"How easy would it be if we were dogs," she said. "Just so happily unaware."

"They know more than we think they know," Jamie said.

"Well, then maybe we should ask him about Lester Hightower."

In his smile, she could see a glimpse of the pre-accident Jamie, the kid whose worst dilemma was deciding which taco to order.

"I think Violet is our key. She can infiltrate."

Sophia made a noise. "Did you really just say infiltrate?"

"I did."

Bailey came up again, apparently tired of running around. The dog made a large sighing noise and curled at their feet.

"Well, whatever happens, I'm glad we're friends again," Sophia said.

Jamie nodded ever so slightly, then said, "Did you like it? With Trevor?"

"You really want to know?"

"No, actually I don't."

"Okay, then. But listen, we should always talk to each other about this stuff, about anything. Just don't try and kiss me."

"Gross!"

Sophia knew he didn't mean that, and so did he, and they both laughed.

Back at the cottage when they parted, Sophia hugged Jamie for a little longer than usual. Bailey let out a jealous whine.

Inside—plopped on the couch and flipping through the channels—Sophia thought about what Jamie had said, about people judging. There was that time in seventh grade, when Quinn Halston, resident mean girl / cheer captain, dropped a banana in her lap during lunch period.

"Your mothers may need that," Quinn had said, the posse of girls around her giggling.

Sophia just sat there, stone cold, staring. She didn't know what to say. So she peeled the banana and started eating it.

Then there was another time, when her mothers were at her soccer game. Sophia was acutely aware of Jocelyn—the goalie, who was in Quinn's posse—watching her mothers and shaking her head, like it was a shame. In their huddle, Jocelyn maneuvered away from Sophia, like her mothers' gayness might have rubbed off on her.

That night, Courtney explained to Sophia what homophobia was and how usually people who didn't like gay people were afraid, either because they didn't understand it or because they felt it themselves. A light went on in Sophia's head, because Jocelyn seemed to carry herself just like her mothers—with confidence, an edge, and a touch of masculinity.

Those two incidents stuck with her, but not much happened after that. Quinn and her posse had bigger fish to fry than some girl with two moms. Sophia was grateful.

After her mothers returned from their cliff walk, the three of them sat down to dinner. About halfway through, Jane turned to Courtney and said, "Someone reunited with a friend today."

"I'm right here, Mom," Sophia said. "I'm not someone."

"Who?" Courtney asked.

"Jamie!" Jane confirmed.

"Oh, that is excellent. He's a great kid. I never understood why you stopped hanging out with him."

*You have no idea*, Sophia didn't say. She agreed with her mothers, but that didn't mean she wanted to talk about it with them. She decided to change the subject. "What do you guys know about Lester Hightower?"

Jane made a face, like she had sipped old orange juice.

"Specifically, in regards to the SEC." Sophia had googled him before dinner and discovered, deep in the comments section of a tweet, that there was some speculation he may be implicated for insider trading regarding JREXX, the stock symbol that Brendan had written in his journal, which was currently under Sophia's bed.

Courtney, who knew all the NYC stockbroker movers and shakers, put down her fork gently and looked at Sophia. "I once went on a boat ride around Manhattan with him."

Jane shot her wife a look.

"Not *with* him—there was maybe, thirty people. I got the sense that he was smart, but oily. Why do you ask?"

Sophia just shrugged her shoulders and took a bite of her fish. It was Jane's special–steamed cod with lemon butter. Despite everything, she felt safe and very much at home in that instant, the flaky fish practically melting on her tongue. Jane didn't eat sugar but she loved butter, the fresh kind from France.

"How's the essay coming?" Jane asked, in her obviously nonchalant way.

"I'm having trouble with it. I was going to write about how I felt when I went to the Brown campus, but that feels too on the nose and like, sycophantic."

"Hmm. What about Letisha?" Courtney asked, referencing one of the inner-city kids Sophia mentored. Letisha didn't talk at all when Sophia first met her. There was "trauma" in her home, as they called it. The first couple times they hung out, they just listened to music, female empowerment type songs from singers like Sara Bareilles and Elle King. Eventually, Letisha—who was a beautiful, wide-eyed child with tight braids—started to loosen up a little. Sophia had been reading about music therapy online. It was working. The third time Letisha came over, Sophia played her violin, a somber but pretty melody she had learned early on. After Sophia finished, the girl spoke.

"Is it hard to play that?"

"I bet it won't be for you. Want me to teach you?"

Letisha smiled, and her whole face came alive.

Maybe Courtney was right. She could write about Letisha, the girl who had completely transformed before her eyes.

"Yeah, that's a good idea," Sophia said, dragging her last bite of fish through the rest of the sauce on her plate.

"So, you'll keep me in the act?" Courtney asked.

Jane laughed and leaned over to kiss Courtney on the cheek. Sometimes Sophia cringed at her mothers' cutesy affection, but tonight she just smiled. She was lucky. She had a nice family. She was going to Brown. Well, unless that secret from last summer caught up to her. Maybe Jamie was right. They needed to nip it in the bud. But how?

She skipped dessert, which was sugar-free ice cream (eww), telling them she needed to work on her essay. They beamed proudly. That was the thing—her mothers loved her, and probably never could imagine she was capable of doing what she and Jamie and Trevor had done. They had zero clue. *How much do we really know about the people who are closest to us? Are there certain things that should never be spoken, stay in the vault forever?* It made Sophia queasy thinking about it.

Back in her room, she got distracted by an instant message ping. It was Lyle, her creepy violin teacher. The message said, *Hey there, how are you doing?*

Sophia typed back:

*Really? U r just going to act like everything is normal?*

His text bubble appeared and retreated a couple times, but ultimately he chickened out.

*You're lucky I didn't tell anyone*, she typed back, and then deleted the thread.

Opening her laptop, she clicked on the file titled "college essay."

*There are moments in time that seem small and insignificant but in fact change everything . . .*

# CHAPTER 10

# JAMIE

His catering gig was at the Miacomet golf club. Jamie was in charge of serving chicken from the heated pans and loading up people's plates with dollops of mashed potatoes and piles of green beans. It was some golf association luncheon, and most of the people were wearing Nantucket red, whale belts, and had sun-kissed skin. Jamie watched Cameron across the room, serving people drinks and smiling in his assured, somewhat geeky way.

After the shift, all the cater waiters and bartenders met in the lounge on the second floor, which was crammed with old leather couches and plaques with the names of golfers who'd won tournaments over the years.

Jamie's boss, Pete—who loved to gossip and had a man bun that a lot of the workers called the "manager bun"—came up behind him and noticed the name on the plaque he was looking at: Lester Hightower.

"You know him?" Pete asked, pointing at the name.

"I know his stepdaughter."

"Violet?"

"Yes."

"Nice girl. I always sensed she doesn't buy Lester's act."

"What do you mean, act?"

Pete chugged the bottle of beer he was holding and shook his head.

"Lester tries to be old money, but he's a different breed. Grew up in Newark. He's basically a grifter who came into a lot of money, most likely in illegal ways."

Jamie thought of the stock symbol written in Brendan's notebook.

"Hmm. Hey, did you know a guy named Brendan?"

Pete sighed and sat down, like this could take a while. Jamie did the same.

"I did. But anything I say is between you and me, kid, got it?"

"Sure."

"From what I understand, Brendan fell under Lester's spell, and it ultimately led to his demise."

"Demise?" Jamie tried to act like this was news to him. "How so?"

"Well, the legend goes that Brendan had a secret on Lester, something about insider trading. You see, Lester had been paying Brendan for odd jobs for years, but it was like, minimum wage. Brendan thought it was time to cash in. So he tried to extort Lester, 'cause he was in the hole for gambling. They got in a fight after a party at Lester's, and this part I'm not sure about, but apparently Lester drugged Brendan, and that's why he drove into a tree."

Jamie felt his lungs expand as he breathed deeply, and he tried to act normal.

"What's wrong?"

"Nothing," Jamie lied. "It's just … someone told me the autopsy said alcohol, but not drugs."

162

Pete finished his beer and set it down on the table between them. "Well, that's where the corruption comes in. You're a smart kid. You know about corruption, right?"

"Yeah. You think Lester paid the cops off?"

"Let's just say Lester's money has relationships with a lot of people. It's sort of a known fact on the island that the guy is a criminal."

"What's your connection?"

"He's hired our company a few times. And I have other clients that know him."

Cameron, who Jamie had briefly forgotten was working the event, walked up and sat down right next to him.

"Hey," he said.

"Hey," Jamie said back.

Pete got a text and left.

"You look like you've seen a ghost," Cameron said.

"Well, I just got some information that may change everything."

"From Pete? He can be quite the talker."

"Yeah. But I liked what he was telling me. I mean, if it's true."

"What did he say?"

Jamie looked at Cameron, and something about the open expression on his face made Jamie want to tell him everything . . . so he did. By the time he was finished, they were the only two left in the lounge.

"Well, let's hope Pete was right," Cameron said. "Gets you and your friends off the hook."

"Exactly."

Cameron smiled and put his hand on Jamie's shoulder.

This was the moment that Jamie couldn't have planned. He leaned in and kissed Cameron, who tasted like citrus and smoke. He could feel a tingling in his fingers and down the length of his spine. Then a swelling all through his chest, like something inside him was breaking through, coming alive.

When they broke apart, Jamie said, "Shit, maybe I'm gay."

Cameron laughed and said, "I did think you were, but my gaydar is not always on point. Especially the time I tried to kiss *you*."

"So, should we sleep together now?"

Cameron laughed again, then said, "Not on the first date. But there's a movie I want to see playing downtown in an hour. I have some time before my ferry. Wanna—"

"Yes," Jamie answered before Cameron even finished asking.

The movie was one of those indies where the characters were charming, quirky, and relatable. A grand romantic gesture three-quarters of the way through made both of them tear up. Afterward, they got pizza slices and sat on a bench watching the lights on the harbor. It seemed, to Jamie, unimaginable. Like some kind of idealistic, utopian moment. The perfect place to be. He knew it was just a crush, but still, he wished that he could bottle the feeling so he could open it up at any time and taste it.

"So, you going to forgive your friends?"

"Well, I already forgave Sophia. Trevor, I don't know. He's like, always been this hero to me I guess. And it's just tainted now. First with the accident, then with him hooking up with Sophia."

"But you didn't have any claim on Sophia, did you?"

"Only as a friend."

"Ah, the friend zone. Know it well."

"He's just been a dick through everything."

"I get it. But holding a grudge can be toxic," Cameron said. "I'm on the team of forgiveness, even though it's hard."

"I guess the person I need to forgive first is myself."

Cameron moved some hair out of Jamie's eyes and said, "Well, that seems like a good plan. And it may be easier than you think, especially if Pete is right. But be careful."

"That's what everyone says."

Cameron checked his phone and said, "Well, I gotta catch my ferry. This was my last shift on the rock. But if you want to come visit me in Boston, you're welcome . . ."

"Really?"

"A hundred percent."

"Good odds."

Cameron kissed him, and Jamie felt the tingling again. He tried to picture the look on his parents' faces if he were to tell them he was gay. They would accept him. They wouldn't care. Maybe everything would be okay. Maybe.

Back in Connecticut a few weeks after the accident, Jamie spent a lot of time wondering how he could even go on. Everything seemed pointless. He basically had a hand in *murdering* someone. He walked around in a muted world; people talked but he couldn't make out the words. His grades started to suffer. Even worse, he was cut off from his two best friends.

He never would have imagined that the person who would pull him out of the darkness would be his seventy-year-old neighbor, Grace, but it was. He was taking out the trash when he heard her call out to him.

"Jamie, is it? Could you be a doll and help me out with something?"

That was it. He nodded, and five minutes later, he was watering a plant Grace couldn't reach, in her kitchen that smelled like lemon and cloves.

When he finished and got down off of her stepladder, she put both her hands on his shoulders and said, "A dumb question—do you like hot chocolate?"

It was Jamie's favorite. Maybe it was his lucky day. He nodded again.

"I make it Mexican style."

He put up his arms and said, "Sounds good."

Turned out the secret ingredient was cinnamon. They sat in her sunroom listening to her old record player. Frank Sinatra. Jamie didn't care for such retro music, but in that setting it worked. In fact, Jamie was just happy to be away from his everyday life. Grace's house had so many memories that weren't his own. Black-and-white pictures of her and her sisters on a beach, African masks on the walls, a typewriter from the fifties sitting next to a vintage sewing machine.

"Do you think I could paint you?"

"What?"

She held up a paintbrush. "I need subjects. Real live ones."

"Um . . ."

"I can pay you. Say, twenty bucks an hour?"

Jamie thought about it for a second. It wasn't creepy. He liked Grace. She wore bright sweaters and a necklace of dented copper. She read the *New York Times* old school—the actual paper, which was stacked all around her house in little piles.

"Why not," Jamie said.

So every Tuesday for the next few months, Jamie sat for Grace. He was worried he'd get too suffocated by his thoughts in such silence, but it was the opposite. While Grace painted, she talked, on and on like a radio with no off switch.

She told him about her father surviving the holocaust, watching children pulled from their mothers, seeing mountains of bodies on the side of the road. It was horrible stuff, but it had helped him to know that there were bad things happening everywhere, unfathomably worse than what was happening to him.

She also told him about her first love, Kurt, who was a jet fighter pilot with what she called "cheek bones that could cut glass." They apparently broke into a bakery late one night and danced, with powdered sugar in clouds around them. Jamie loved her details. He planned on doing a piece on her in the school newspaper, maybe even submitting it to a national magazine. Each time he came home, he'd write down notes.

Jamie's parents were supportive of his new friendship with Grace, but they, too, seemed to be orbiting in their own worlds. His father worked all the time, and his mother had a rigid exercise routine when she wasn't being a part-time hospital administrator. There was a time when he talked to his mother, even his father, about anything, but that time had passed. He loved them, but confessing was not an option. It was like they went through the world parallel now, his parents and him, never fully facing each other. Maybe it was a dance and eventually they would turn, cross lines. But for now it was stick to your lane.

So he told Grace. Or rather, Grace got it out of him.

On a rainy Tuesday, as she painted, Jamie stared at the water dripping down her windows. The world's tears.

"There is something dark in you," she said. "A secret? I'm afraid I can't paint that out of your face. Do you want to tell me what it is?"

"It's going to sound stupid."

"That's what they all say," Grace said.

Jamie smiled, and again figured, *Why not*. He had to tell someone. So he did, and she didn't seem shocked. In fact, she even laughed a little. That hurt, because Jamie didn't think it was funny at all.

"Do you really think an egg would cause a crash?" Grace asked.

"Well, either that or it was extremely coincidental."

"Why didn't you report it?"

"Trevor. He made us all stay silent."

"And no one has suspected you?"

"Not yet."

"Well, no news is good news."

Jamie sighed. It was a simple statement, but maybe she was right.

Three Tuesdays later, when Jamie saw Grace's finished painting of him, his heart pumped in his throat. She had made him look older, or more masculine somehow. And she was right, the secret was there, right in his face—a part of his skin, and coming out of his eyes. He was emanating it.

In the following months he saw Grace regularly, but she didn't paint him. They'd just drink hot chocolate and talk. Jamie wrote the story about her for the school newspaper and brought her a copy. She read it in front of him, her eyes pooling with water. Three tissues later, she was finished.

"I'm not that great, am I?" Grace asked.

"You have no idea," Jamie said. He submitted it to the *New Yorker* the next day.

Now, watching the workers getting Cameron's ferry ready to leave the harbor, he had an impulse to run up and jump on, to follow Cameron to Boston, to be bold and impulsive like Grace. Break into a bakery. Dance under clouds of powdered sugar.

Instead, Jamie got on the bus, which on Nantucket was a glorified van they called *The Wave*. He noticed the people sitting across from him. They were workers, like him. They had struggles, like him. It was important to feel that he was not alone in this. He was starting to understand that he wasn't. He had Sophia and Violet and Cameron, even though he was on a boat motoring away as each minute passed. He even had Trevor, if he wanted. He still wasn't sure about that.

# CHAPTER 11

# VIOLET

In her swimming dream, everything was the same except there was someone else in the water, chasing her on a Jet Ski. She swam faster and faster, and even though the island stayed far in the distance, each time she looked back the Jet Ski got closer. She went under, hoping it would zoom by, but when she surfaced, it was right behind her—driven by Lester, who was laughing hysterically. He circled her and then sped off, dunking her in his wake, leaving her stranded in the middle of the sea. She sunk farther down, giving up. Right before she hit the bottom, she woke up.

After reading the litany of texts from Jamie that came in over the night, she googled the symbol JREXX. There were two people linked to the company who were charged with insider trading, and one of them Violet remembered Lester talking about: Elliot Marsden. She went downstairs and downed some orange juice, noticing the note on the kitchen table. Her mother was playing golf, and Lester's Range Rover wasn't in the driveway. Even Ricardo, who was omnipresent in the household, was nowhere to be found. It must have been his day off. Since the coast seemed pretty clear, she went into Lester's library office and opened his laptop. Her first try at a password worked. Of course Lester would be dumb enough to use his old dog's name,

Rocket, as his password. The dog he never stopped talking about. She opened up his contacts and typed in the name Elliot, and a ton of emails came up. All of them were dated before June 12 last year; after Elliot was charged, there was no contact. Clicking through, the emails all seemed like normal business correspondence, except for one random one, where the language was cryptic. Violet searched the symbol JREXX, and an additional slew of emails surfaced. There seemed to be a lot of sent emails from Lester with the symbol in the body of the email. Some of them had been deleted from the server but still had time stamps—all leading up to the day the stock went public. She decided to search the date of Brendan's death, just to see. The emails were regular, except for one: a receipt from what looked like an online pharmacy. It appeared Lester was asking some phony doctor, maybe on the dark web, where he could get something called GHB. She googled the letters, quickly finding out it was a "date rape" drug. She shuddered, her eyes pulsing at the screen. Was Lester actually capable of this?

She closed his mail folder and put the computer to sleep, just like how she found it. A screen saver showed an animated shark swimming across the screen with blood dripping from its mouth. Of course it did. What a scumbag.

With her hand still on the mouse, she heard the front door slam in the distance and then someone hiss at her from the doorway of the office.

"Babygirl! What are you doing?" It was Ricardo, flapping his arms, motioning for her to get out of there.

She could feel her heartbeat pulsing in her temples, and actually started giggling with nerves as she sprinted past Ricardo down the hall and out the back door, not stopping until she was on the steps. The ocean churned, reflecting the sun with its endless glinting and shimmering. It looked so beautiful on its surface, but underneath unfathomable things lurked—sharks, blood, animalistic greed.

She texted Jamie right away.

*Can you come to my steps now?*

He texted right back.

*Sure thing*

Violet turned and look toward the house. She didn't even want to go back there. What if Lester planned on drugging *her*? She shivered at the thought.

Jamie arrived a few minutes later, panting.

"Are you okay?" he asked.

"Yes. But this whole thing is a rabbit hole. Insider trading, and now GHB."

Jamie shook his head and whispered, "Oh my god."

"What?"

"It's exactly what my boss said. What about the autopsy?"

"I checked. GHB leaves the body in twelve hours. It's highly unlikely they did an autopsy that quickly. They put emergencies before anything else . . . like murders."

"That's ironic."

"Tell me about it."

"So what are you going to do?"

"I don't know. I'm like, shaking."

Violet showed Jamie her hand, and Jamie held it.

"No cameras?"

"Not in Lester's office. Only outside."

They sat on the bench, watching the ocean, waiting for some horror to reveal itself, like a monster breaking through the surface But it was just that beautiful blue green, with birds and fishing boats loafing about.

"Look, I have to go to work," Jamie said. "But we have to try and prove this somehow."

"I know. I think Ricardo might be the key."

"Well, just be extra careful. Try and avoid Lester."

"I will."

Jamie hugged her pretty tightly, and it felt good to know someone cared. Her mother was delusional, her father was disconnected, and her stepfather was . . . possibly a murderer. Her prospects weren't great.

She tiptoed to her room, and once inside, quietly locked her bedroom door and called her father, who barely even used his phone. It was one of those annoying generic messages, and she was impatient, so she hung up. Then she called him right back and this time waited for the computer voice to finish and the beep to sound.

"Hey, Dad, it's me, Violet. I hope you are doing well . . ."

Her voice sounded fake, like a carbon copy of itself.

"Listen, I need to talk to you . . ."

It was devastating to be talking to a device with no one on the other end, but she had to. She could feel hot tears burning behind her eyes.

"There's something going on. I mean, I'm not sure if it's safe here. Lester is . . . Lester may be a bad person, Dad, like, a really bad person… There's some information I found out about Brendan, the guy who worked for him … the one who died …"

A message came on asking if she was done recording or wanted to continue. She hit 2 to continue.

"Dad, I don't know what to do. I wish you were here. Anyway, I love you."

She meant it. She did love him. His mental illness wasn't his fault. Back in the days when he was happy, he'd been a good father. Telling her story after story off the top of his head when she couldn't sleep, teaching her how to sail in the little Sunfish, telling her she was the prettiest little girl in the world.

"Ok, bye …"

○ ○ ○

Violet was officially scared to be in her own house. But she had to eat, and she was relieved to see Ricardo in the kitchen. Violet made herself a sandwich, and Ricardo fixed her an iced tea.

"This isn't drugged, is it?" Violet asked.

Ricardo rolled his eyes.

"Babygirl, why don't you channel some of your imagination into your music?"

"I do have a new song. It's called 'Snake in the Garden.'"

Ricardo sighed, then went back to wiping the counter.

Violet's mother walked in right then, looking flushed and scattered. She drank some water in front of the sink, then turned around and stared at Violet.

"Are you going to do something this summer?"

"Mom, I told you, I'm working on songwriting."

"Have you been sailing with the kids?"

"Yes, but last time it was canceled 'cause of the rain."

Her mother made a puffing noise, like Violet had ordered the weather herself. Then she put her water glass down and left the kitchen. Discussion over. Violet wondered if the facade her mother had worked so hard to build was starting to crumble. She could almost see it in her skin, her posture. All the money in the world didn't solve every problem. It didn't kill the snake in the garden . . . the shark in the sea.

On her way upstairs, Violet could hear Lester and her mother arguing in the den. Something told her to walk up to the door to see if she could hear anything.

"The FBI, Lester. They are calling me."

"No one is going to find out," Lester spat.

"They already have!"

Her mother was crying now, and as much as Violet wanted to comfort her and somehow keep her safe, she was scared of what Lester might do if the situation escalated. Instead, she ran upstairs and locked the door to her room, this time not being quiet about it.

Her mother was not the person she had been with Violet's father. They had money then, but it wasn't so ostentatious. They had a small cottage near Surfside, not a five-bedroom house on Baxter Road. Her mother liked to dress up once in a while, but Violet's father owned only one suit. They didn't have a need to show the world how wealthy they were. She hardly even played tennis. She certainly had never gotten Botox. It's as if Lester and his money was a disease, and now it was spreading into her whole family.

She thought of their neighbors, the ones who never smiled,

and then their neighbors on the other side, who barely used their house. She needed some kind of backup just in case something happened. Then it hit her—Trevor was only three houses down. She texted him casually, to see what he was up to.

*Living the dream,* Trevor typed back.

Violet started to text him back, but where would she start? Thankfully, as if hearing her thoughts, another text came in from him.

*R u ok?*

*Not really*

*Is it your stepdad?*

*Yeah*

*U want to meet*

*Not now but can we have a 911 word*

*??*

*like if there's an emergency, can I text u a word?*

*of course, what will it be?*

*Donut*

*Lol ok*

*It's not funny*

*Look, I saved a kid yesterday—u say donut and I will crush it. I'm not afraid of him.*

His words actually soothed her. Even though she rolled her eyes a lot and used to call him Pretty Boy, the fact was she and Trevor had a lot in common. They were broken.

*I know, sorry*

*It's ok*

*this is going to sound weird, but can I sing to you?*

*what?*

*there's this song my nanny used to sing to me. it's in Swahili. it's the closest thing to xanax*

Violet smiled. She brushed her teeth, got into her oversized T-shirt, and then crawled under her big, fluffy duvet.

*Ok, ready*

She could never have imagined what unfolded. Trevor calling her, singing an African song. His voice so close in her ear, like he was there in the room. It was so unexpected, and so beautiful, that she started to cry. The tears weren't necessarily from joy, but maybe partly. It was all the emotions—fear, anger, and maybe, for a kid she barely knew, love.

## CHAPTER 12

# TREVOR

He remembered the song. It was ingrained in his very essence, that song. Bea, his nanny, had sung it to him throughout his childhood.

*Jambo, jambo bwana*
*habari gani*
*Jambo, jambo bwana*
*habari gani*

When he sang it to Violet, whom he no longer thought of as the Hightower stepdaughter but someone luminous in her beauty and mystery, he forgot the last section of words so he just made them up. Thankfully, she didn't notice, but when he hung up the phone he found himself giggling.

It's not that his parents didn't love him. They certainly did, in their way. But Bea was the one who had bathed and clothed him, took him to preschool, the park, his playdates. She sang to him almost every night, and she had the most beautiful smile—surprising, like Violet's. Once a year for a month, she would go back to Uganda, and Trevor remembered those months feeling like a year. As he got older and made friends, Bea receded from his life, but never fully. When he thought of what love was, it was her image that floated into his head—the soothing sound of her voice, the soft touch of her hands.

One day, when he was twelve, she left for Africa and never came back. Trevor had been so pissed at his parents for not telling him she was gone for good, he insisted they go visit her the following year. His parents shunned the idea at first, but eventually they caved. On his thirteenth birthday, Trevor had flown to Uganda. He'd stepped on the sacred earth, seen elephants in the wild, heard the symphony of animal sounds at night. Though he and his parents stayed at a hotel in the main city, they went to visit Bea's house in a small village on the outskirts. Trevor felt embarrassed to his core, and grossly superior somehow, when he discovered she lived on the second floor of what could only be described as a hut, above two goats and a sickly chicken. Here was the woman who had raised him in Connecticut, the epicenter of white privilege, living in what Trevor knew was well below the poverty line. But even as his parents were silently judging the situation, Trevor was young enough to just dial in to their energy. Bea and her father were so proud, so unmasked. He remembered being thrilled, but also a little scared. They all walked into what was considered a town, but really it was a couple of trailers that served food on the side of the dusty street. His parents were clearly uncomfortable, and he told them to chill. The street food they all ate was warm homemade bread with eggs and tomatoes and cabbage. He could've eaten that for days.

When Trevor hugged Bea goodbye, they both had a hard time looking each other in the eye. How could they? What does ten years of emotion look like in someone's eyes? How do you quantify a decade of being so close, yet so far apart? It was overwhelming. On the way back to the Sheraton, his parents had tried to talk to him, but he couldn't even make out their words. He wasn't listening. He'd just had his mind blown.

● ● ●

On the way into town, he drove past the "Serengeti"—a section of land off of Milestone Road with two trees in the distance on the horizon, that everyone said looked like Africa. It did, but not really. It wasn't the same feeling he'd had in Africa, eating that simple but wonderful meal with Bea's family on that Ugandan street corner. It was like being connected to everyone and everything.

As he had many times, Trevor wondered where Bea was right now. He'd last heard she ran a small textile company and had a daughter. *I will find her one day*, Trevor thought.

When he pulled into Bryce's driveway, a nervous-looking Alison came outside before Trevor could get out of the car. He rolled down the window.

"Did you guys get caught in a riptide?" she asked.

Trevor had to decide right then, in the blink of an eye, what to do. Play it down? Go for the whole truth?

"No, just a small current."

Alison sighed and wiped her brow with the sleeve of her Lululemon pullover. "Okay, you know he has quite the imagination, and I believe about half of what he says."

"Yeah."

"But maybe just Children's Beach for the rest of the summer?"

Trevor opened the door, and Alison scooted back to let him out.

"No problem, you got it."

She smiled, and everything seemed normal again. Crisis averted. When they got inside, Alison suggested he and Bryce go for a walk, so that's what they did. Trevor was happy to see Bryce looked more like a kid today—hair sticking up, Disney T-shirt, flip-flops. Usually he was in seersucker shorts and a collared shirt, which was cute and all, but a bit much.

They walked to the juice bar and got ice cream cones, then started zigzagging the docks, passing sailboats, fishing charters, and the occasional yacht.

"Do you think from the sky all these docks look like letters that spell a word?" Bryce asked.

Trevor never thought of it that way. "Maybe. What word would it spell?"

"Well, there are no curved docks, so not a lot of vowels."

Where did this kid get this stuff? Did Trevor ever have that creative of a brain? When he was Bryce's age, he drew a lot; but when he started playing sports, art went out the window. Maybe he could try it again, now that sports (at least team ones) were out the window.

Brent, one of Trevor's surfing buddies, walked by with two dudes he'd never met. They all had worn baseball hats on and board shorts.

"Babysitting now? Isn't that a girl's job?" Brent mocked.

"Shut up," Trevor said.

The three guys laughed as they walked away.

Bryce sighed and said, "Bullies are insecure."

Trevor laughed a little and said, "Probably."

"Plus, it's not babysitting because I'm not a baby."

"What would you call it?" Trevor asked.

"Professional childcare," Bryce said, like he had coined the phrase.

"That sounds good. Or how about, kickin' it with my buddy?"

Bryce got a worried look on his face for a second, like Trevor had crossed some boundary, but then he smiled and they clinked ice cream cones.

He could see a girl rigging a Sunfish below them in the water. As he got closer he realized it was Violet. Trevor suddenly felt like he was in seventh grade. WTF?

She waved, her skin glistening in the sun.

"Hey, thanks for last night," she said.

"Sure." Trevor could feel his face heating up.

"Is this something I shouldn't be hearing about?" Bryce asked.

Trevor laughed, then introduced the kid to Violet.

"I just sang her a song, buddy," Trevor said.

"Seriously?" Bryce was skeptical. Then he said, "Okay, we'll go with that."

Violet laughed.

"Hey, I have to finish getting the boat ready for the kids I volunteer for. But I'll call you later."

"Cool, sounds good."

As they walked away, Bryce said, "She's really pretty."

"Yeah," Trevor said. "She sure is."

Trevor stopped by Serge's boat after taking Bryce back home. It seemed more spacious, like Serge had cleaned it up a little.

"Tell me, young man, what are you smiling about?"

Trevor hadn't realized he was smiling.

Serge handed him a beer, but Trevor shook his head.

"Coke?" Serge offered.

"Sure."

"I should too. It's a bit early."

They sat in silence for a few minutes, listening to some fishermen haggling about prices in the distance.

"It's a girl," Serge said, like it was obvious.

"Yep."

"Here we go."

"She's different, Serge. Like, crazy beautiful. I just never noticed it before."

"That's 'cause your head's up your ass."

"Shut up."

"You are waking up. Seeing the glimpse of a great romance. Being in love is a time when we feel alive the most."

Trevor sighed. "I don't even know if she likes me. I mean, there's something there . . ." He couldn't believe he was even talking about this. In the past, he never had an issue around girls. If he wanted one, he could have one. Not take one, have one—served to him on a silver platter. It was gross to think about. He felt his face flush with shame.

"Well, if you love her you must tell her. These are the decisions that can change the course of your whole life. Look at me, I ended up on a never-ending ocean ride."

"That doesn't sound too bad."

Serge sipped his Coke, shook his head. "I made a lot of mistakes, kid. A lot. It's not the *one* who got away for me . . . it's they *all* got away."

Trevor smiled. "Well, you still got time. You're only what, sixty?"

Serge mimed impaling himself with a sword. "Fifty-four."

"Even better."

Trevor downed the rest of his soda and got up and stretched on the bow.

"Go get her," Serge said.

"Maybe. First I'm gonna surf."

Back in his Jeep, on his way out the long, bumpy dirt road, Trevor couldn't get the image of Violet out of his head. The way she rigged the sail like she'd been doing it forever. Her perfect skin, her elegant lips, her stunning brown eyes.

The waves were pretty decent at Nobadeer Beach. He saw Brent, the dick who gave him a hard time at the docks, and purposely walked to the far side. The surf was stronger there anyway. On his first wave, and his second, he thought about nothing but that very moment. The rush and the speed, the water sparkling all around him. On his third ride, he thought of Violet, waving from her boat. She had looked ethereal, like he'd seen a different side of the female species.

The sky turned a little, and the waves got bigger. He was getting pretty tired, so he told himself this next one would be his last. He waited until he could see a huge swell growing. He knew it was big, maybe in the top five biggest he'd ever rode. He popped up and steadied himself, the board gaining momentum, shredding the water, chasing the curl. But the wave rose even higher, and now he was going too fast, and it was too late. The sheer force of the wave propelled him forward.

He roared like some kind of animal, his voice echoing into

the sky. His board jerked to the left and sailed off, and he lost his footing.

In a split second he, too, was in the air, flying backward with his board next to him. He put his arms up and tried to duck as the board flew toward him, but it happened way too fast and he couldn't get out of the way in time. It smacked him right on the back of his head.

The next thing he saw was the board again, this time underneath the water. He reached for it, grabbing hold, pulling himself toward it. Then everything went black.

He woke to the sting and hiss of the fluorescent light above him. There was a cheesy print on the wall of—believe it or not—an ocean wave. He was in a hospital bed. His mother was sitting at his side, a tear running down from each eye. It was kind of beautiful, or maybe he was just drugged out. What had they given him?

"Mom?"

"You had an accident, Turtle."

He usually hated when she called him that, but right now he was grateful. Someone out there in the world was there for him, had known he was obsessed with turtles (even though Bea was the one who used to take him to Greenwich pond to see them).

"Jesus, Trevor. You almost gave me a heart attack. The lifeguards called an ambulance, because you weren't making sense when you came to."

"Oh."

It was coming back to him a little. He remembered another

surfer helping him. Was it Brent? And also some blond dude dumping a bottle of water over his face.

"You okay now?"

Trevor thought about it. Aside from his head swirling a little, he seemed fine. "Yeah, I think."

His mother started crying some more. She was always so perfect, so put together, but right then she looked grotesque.

"I'm fine, Mom, I'm fine. Stop."

"Your father's in Tokyo. I haven't been able to reach him."

"Don't. It's fine. The swell was too big. I knew it, but something told me to go for it."

They looked at each other, and she smiled, like maybe she was just a little proud.

"Do you have my board?" Trevor asked.

She laughed a little through her tears. "Yes, Turtle, but can we take a break from surfing, just for a while?"

Trevor knew that wouldn't happen, but he nodded silently to appease her.

They fed him tomato soup and grilled cheese, and it tasted heavenly, like he hadn't eaten in days. The doctor—a stern woman with severe black bangs—told him they needed to run a few more tests on him before they could release him, that it may be a day or two. She said as far as she could tell he was very lucky.

*Lucky*, Trevor thought. *Yes, and no.*

"There's one thing," his mother said after the doctor left. "The first responder, she said you kept repeating a name, over and over. Brendan?"

Trevor's heart did a little dance underneath his hospital gown. He had never consciously said the guy's name out loud.

"Who's Brendan?" he asked, but his voice cracked.

"I was hoping you'd tell me. You said that you needed to see him."

Trevor could feel his blood heating up, pulsing through him. "I don't know, Mom, honestly. I don't know what I was talking about. Just forget it, okay?"

"Okay, okay. I'm just glad you're all right."

When she and the nurse left the room and Trevor was all alone, he wept, but not silently like he had in the bathroom at Violet's house. No, this was an uncontrollable, heaving kind of cry. He tried not to be too loud, but he had to let it go. Maybe that was what Electra had been talking about.

When he finally calmed down, he took some breaths and wiped his face with his gown. He was calling Brendan's name? This thing had to go away, somehow. Facing the rest of his life branded by it, like a tattoo on his soul, seemed impossible. And he was glad to be alive. Lucky, even.

He was released from the hospital the next day. When they got home, they sat on the couch. Trevor couldn't remember the last time his mother had hugged him, but there she was, holding him. Electra brought them a pitcher of water with lemon slices in a little fish-shaped bowl.

"You realize," Trevor said, "we're the type of people that always have lemon in our water?"

"What?"

"Nothing."

She held him closer and stroked his hair, and though it felt strange and new, he liked it. There was a time, maybe when he was twelve, that Trevor decided it was uncool to be the object of his mother's affection. Now, he wasn't so sure. He had plenty of money, but affection wasn't as easy to come by.

"So, I was thinking, Mom," Trevor said, even though the idea had just occurred to him, "of taking a gap year."

He expected her to balk, but she just stared into the distance with a slight smile. She didn't say anything for a while, and he could smell the bleach from her tennis top. Finally, she let him go, stood up, and walked toward the window, then turned around.

"I took a gap year, you know," she said proudly.

"What? I didn't know that. What did you do?"

"I went to Europe."

"I'm thinking Costa Rica. Remember Dylan?"

"Your old surf instructor?"

"Yeah. He has a kiteboarding school there."

"Hmm."

"I don't know. I mean, I'll see how it goes, but I may just want some time to figure it all out."

"I get it, but let's not tell your father just yet, okay?"

"Yeah. That's like, the one thing he cares about—me going to college."

"Trevor, that's not fair."

"A lot of things aren't fair."

Trevor wanted to list those things, the reasons why his own father was such a dickhead, but it wasn't the time. Besides, his mother knew them firsthand.

Her phone buzzed.

"I have to take this. I've canceled my dinner, so I'll be here if you need me, okay?"

Trevor waved her off and walked up to his room. Considering he'd just blacked out and been in the hospital overnight, he felt pretty good. He took a shower, thinking again about Violet on the boat, how her skin practically glowed and her smile changed her whole face. As he toweled off, he looked at himself in the mirror. He tried to see what Violet did. Someone worthy? Someone guilty?

He texted Sophia. No response.

He texted Jamie. No response.

But he knew where they were.

He just knew.

# CHAPTER 13

# SOPHIA

Waiting in line with her finger paints at the Sconset market, Sophia was giddy. She was about to do something really risky, but it seemed inevitable, like the only solution to a problem that had been bugging her for a while. Every time she tried to answer the prompt on the Brown application essay (*What makes you unique?*), it came out like a high school cliché-fest and just lame. The story about Letisha was promising, but it didn't really answer the prompt. She thought of telling the whole story about the eggs, the car, and Brendan, in a masked way, but she didn't know how that was going to end. She was grateful when another idea had come to her the minute she'd woken up that morning, and it was decided.

On the way home, Bailey kept looking up at her like he knew something was going on—that little tilt of his head and the gleam in his eyes. Dogs could sense things much deeper than humans could. Jamie had once told her that.

The night of the accident, Sophia had gone down into their basement to cry in the damp, dark cement cave that smelled like mildew. She had heard a scratching at the basement door. It was Bailey. She let him down, and he sat right next to her until she was silent. He rested his snout on Sophia's knee and kept it there. She never loved anything more than Bailey at that moment.

Now, back at the cottage, she printed out the application old-school style and filled everything in. It was all impressive: her grades, extracurricular, violin. It was just the essay that was still an empty page. But she was about to change all that.

She closed the door to her room and wondered what paint to choose. Red, definitely. It was the color of passion, desire. She poured the paint onto a paper plate and then very carefully dipped her open palm into it, making an imprint on the page where her essay should have been. It looked like a first-grade art project, but she had to admit, it was a good idea. What else would show, so directly and simply, how unique she was? It was avant-garde. She would one day tell her grandkids about it. While she waited for it to dry, Bailey loped in, looking for affection. She almost started petting him with her red hand, but stopped herself, giggling.

"I did it, Bailey. I've committed. Or maybe I should be committed. I may have just annihilated my collegiate career, but at least they'll remember me."

Bailey whined as if to say, *How could anyone not?*

It dried very quickly, and before she could second-guess herself, she put the entire application in a manila envelope and marched to the Sconset post office, which was in a tiny old building by the rotary. There was one window, and it was rarely open. She waited in line for like, ten minutes, and when she got to the front, she realized she had no money on her. Was this a sign? Should she rethink this idea? Then, as an answer to her question, a lovely old woman behind her put her hand on Sophia's shoulder and said, "I'll cover it, dear."

"Thank you!" Sophia said, relieved she could just be done

with it. All she had to do now was walk out of the post office into the world . . . and wait.

The sun pierced into her skull behind her eyes. What had she done? She felt a buzz and looked down at her phone. It was a text from Jamie, asking to meet somewhere, and she texted him back *yes* before even knowing where. But she had a feeling. It was the place they always met on the down low: the boat graveyard. She took *The Wave* to mid-island and walked down the dirt road to the big doors. Inside, Jamie was sitting in an old rowboat, looking at his phone. When he looked up and saw her, his face lit up.

"Hey!"

"Hi."

For some reason, after sending in such a daring college essay to her dream school, she felt like she could do anything, like all the usual rules were out the window. And Jamie looked absolutely adorable at that moment, something she hadn't fully recognized until right then.

"I know I said we shouldn't kiss ever, but I guess we can, for practice."

"Really?" Jamie was turning red.

Sophia leaned in and kissed him before he could say whatever he was about to say. He tasted like that licorice he always ate, and he wasn't that bad of a kisser. She knew it wasn't her destiny to be with Jamie, but right then, with the sound of the distant waves and the faint smell of boat paint in the air, she felt like everything had led up to that moment.

When they finished, she said, "You know, you're pretty good at that. Maybe you should kiss Cameron."

"What if I already did?"

Sophia's high spirits took a nosedive. Was even Jamie, innocent of all innocents, coming of age? She couldn't fathom him not being like a little brother, someone who would always stand by her, reciting weird facts. As if he heard her thoughts, he said, "Lips are like snowflakes. No two impressions are the same."

Sophia shook her head. How was Jamie so lost but also so tuned-in at the same time? She knew right then that what she had done on the Brown application was right. It was going to work—it had to. As for their predicament, she still wasn't sure.

"What's going on with Operation Freedom?"

It was something they had come up with over text, a kind of code word for figuring out the whole Brendan thing and getting them off the hook.

Jamie filled Sophia in on everything he knew that she didn't.

It all seemed promising, but she was still afraid of Lester. Everyone was. Except maybe Trevor, because he wasn't really afraid of anyone. Sophia liked that about him, but she also knew his bravado wasn't based on anything concrete. Trevor still had to build the foundation he was standing on.

Speak of the devil.

Trevor walked up to them right at that moment, saying, "Thought you guys would be here."

Sophia and Jamie didn't say anything, just stared at him with blank faces.

"Look, you guys. I know I screwed up, and you shouldn't have listened to me, either of you. But a lot has happened. This kid that I babysit, Bryce, I saved him from a riptide. Then I got into a surfing accident, totally blacked out. Anyway, the point is, we need each other."

"What about when I needed you?" Jamie asked.

Sophia added, "Yeah," even though she'd abandoned Jamie too.

"That was the past. You have to believe me when I say I'm different now."

A silence descended as they all thought about that—Trevor, being different.

*He does look different*, Sophia thought. *Humbled, somehow.*

"Okay, so what's the plan?" Jamie asked.

Based on everything they knew, the three of them decided they would have to act. Trevor texted Violet, who was down at the docks in town. She texted back that her parents were both off island, and that Ricardo was about to go shopping. There was a window of time they could check the house for any signs of GHB or anything that would incriminate Lester. She texted Trevor the code to the lockbox.

"Well, I see it hasn't taken you long to get close to Violet," Sophia said, but she was just teasing. Hooking up with Trevor seemed like a lifetime ago. What she wanted now was to be done with it. To be exonerated.

The three of them got into Trevor's Jeep and went to Violet's house. They got in easily, and as promised, no one was there.

Lester's office smelled like cologne and cigars. It was the opposite of all the feminine smells Sophia had grown up with. She kind of liked it, but she didn't tell Jamie or Trevor that.

They snooped around but didn't find anything. Sophia heard a door slam and ran out to the hallway to check. It was a cleaning company, three women with all their supplies, coming toward her.

"Guys, it's the cleaners!" she whispered into the office.

"Tell them they don't need to clean in here!" Trevor whispered back.

Sophia shut the door. The women were now in front of her, giving her a strange look. She started talking to them in Spanish, their native language, and immediately they seemed to be put at ease. She explained to them that the office was off-limits.

"Sí, sí," one of them said and then motioned for the other two to follow her.

Back inside the office, Trevor and Jamie were still looking around.

They checked in between books, inside drawers, even in the trash can. Sophia watched them, wondering if this could be breaking and entering. She could definitely forget college then.

"Look, we should get out of here," Sophia said. In order to not all be seen by the cleaners, they waited, the distant sound of the vacuum and furniture-moving in the background. Jamie's phone buzzed, and he got up quickly, knocking over a wooden owl, which landed heavily on the ground and rolled right over to Sophia's feet. She started to pick it up and put it back, but in the process realized there was a rubber stopper on the bottom, like a piggy bank. She pulled it off, and out dropped a vial of liquid. The label had been scratched. The three of them stared at it, no one moving, barely breathing.

Jamie took a picture of the vial and then started to put it back into the owl.

"Wait! Wipe off your fingerprints!" Sophia said, a little too loudly.

"Is everything okay in there?" called a voice in the hallway, one of the cleaners.

"Yep, everything's fine," Sophia called back.

The three of them froze until they heard the cleaner retreating.

Trevor helped Jamie wipe the vial with the bottom of his T-shirt. Then, as Sophia stood watch in the hallway, one by one they made it out the back door. In the backyard, some workers were already setting up the tent for the party on Friday. Unlike the cleaners, the workers didn't even notice them. Sophia was glad they were all together. Trevor was right; they needed each other.

It was approaching dusk, and the stars started to peek out of the sky, blinking and burning.

Down at the beach, they sat in a circle and didn't say anything for a few minutes, listening to the lapping of the waves and a child crying in the distance.

"Even if that is the GHB, we can't prove it was in Brendan's system," Jamie said.

"Yes, but if it is GHB, it's clearly illegal," Sophia said, "so maybe it's enough to get the cops to look into it."

"The question is, do we go to Lester's party on Friday?" Trevor asked.

"Yes," Sophia and Jamie said together. For a second, it was like nothing bad had happened. Three friends sitting on a beach.

"Okay," Trevor said. "We go to the party and then what?"

"Maybe we can get him on voice memo, saying something about it," Jamie suggested.

"That could work," Sophia said, and both Jamie and Trevor nodded.

Jamie was really bent on doing something. They all were. But for now, there was nothing to do but return to their perspective houses.

Sophia really did miss them all being together. She started to feel tears forming in her eyes but blinked them away.

"Look, no matter what happens, can we officially be friends again?" Trevor asked.

Sophia and Jamie looked at each other in a flash and then turned to Trevor and both said, "Yes."

Trevor let out a *whoop* and ran off toward his house.

Sophia looked at Jamie, who was fully smiling now.

"Don't tell anyone we kissed," she said.

"Why, are you embarrassed?"

"No! But it sounds like you're into Cameron, anyway. And there are enough rumors about me."

"Okay."

She ruffled his hair before they parted. Walking back to her cottage, she found herself smiling. The thing was, she didn't care about the rumors anymore. She was her own person. She was a hand on a page, that looked like no other. She wanted to own it. Life was spreading out before her, and she was looking forward to living it. If they could just get past this one hurdle.

When she got home, she went to her room and started scrolling Twitter feeds, her addiction. About an hour later, Jane came to the door of her room and asked, "Hey, did you send in the Brown app?"

"I did," Sophia replied.

"What did you end up writing about?" Jane wanted to know.

"It's a secret," Sophia said, almost adding *one of many.*

# CHAPTER 14

# VIOLET

Her swimming dream was different this time. The island with the broccoli trees actually got closer, and when she walked on the sand, it didn't give. It was real earth, holding her up. She reached her arms up toward the sun, waiting for something horrible to happen, but it was just beauty. A place of peaceful beauty. She briefly wondered if she had died. Then she woke up.

After a long shower, she put her favorite white dress on, the one her mother had bought her in a rare moment of bonding. They both liked the dress, which had tiny red hearts stitched into the collar. It was technically a "peasant" dress, but she loved the ease of it. She picked out a pencil for her hair, put it up, then applied some lip gloss. Whatever was going down tonight, she was going to look good doing it.

Her phone buzzed—a text from Trevor.

She stared at the message in disbelief. It was the email address of Meghan Trainor's manager. Violet finally had two songs she thought were strong enough to share. She knew they were raw, and only recorded by her phone, but she felt like the lyrics spoke beyond that. She attached the songs to an outgoing email. The first one, "A Real Gentleman," was about her father leaving and also about her ex-boyfriend Chad. How boys and men can be everything but also let you down. The second one, "Snake in the Garden," was about Lester and how sometimes you can't see what's right in front of you. They both had musical hooks that Violet thought were catchy. She introduced herself in the email and thought about the man in the store who had sold her the ukulele when she wrote, *Writing songs gives me life.* After she hit send and heard the swoosh sound, she smiled and shook her head. It was a long shot, obviously, but the good part was that she was actually doing it. No matter who liked it or didn't, she was putting herself out there.

Violet glanced at her watch. People would be arriving in an hour. She knew about the vial of liquid in the owl. The four of them were going to try to incriminate Lester somehow, but they didn't really have an exact plan, other than meeting on the beach stairs.

She went to get her scarf in the laundry room and saw Ricardo, folding clothes with a worried look on his face.

"What?" Violet asked, arranging her scarf in her reflection in the window.

"I overheard you guys. You cannot just go after Lester."

"What else are we going to do?"

"You are pushing it."

"Exactly."

Ricardo stopped folding and turned to Violet. "What if I offered to show you something that might help you?"

"I'd say yes, please."

"Well, I'm not sure if it will help you or not, but whatever you do just be careful. He is not a man to play games with."

"See? I knew you were on to it too."

Ricardo pulled up a video on his phone. "I'm going to erase this," he said, "but I will let you see it so you guys can have a wake-up call as to who you are actually dealing with."

He pressed play. First it was just black, but she could hear voices. Then the point of view changed, like it was filmed through a slightly opened door. It was not a clear view, but she could tell it was Lester, dipping two drops from a vial into a glass of scotch. He then handed it to someone, saying, "Have some of this. We'll figure it all out, don't worry." You could only see the receiving person's arm, but of course it was Brendan. Then the screen went black.

Her breath stopped.

"Ricardo, you need to save this."

He put the phone back into his pocket. "I will delete it later."

"I'm afraid your plan backfired. Now we *have* to confront him."

Ricardo threw up his hands, as if it was in God's hands now.

"Don't worry," Violet said, kissing him on the cheek. "We won't do anything stupid."

"Famous last words," Ricardo said, rolling his eyes.

Back in her room, she texted Trevor and Jamie about the video. She didn't have Sophia's number, but she told them to keep her in the loop. They both texted back emojis—a wow face and an anger face.

Then she texted Ricardo.

*Send me the video, then erase our thread. I won't say where I got it, I promise.*

He started to text back, and she waited, saying *pleeeease* under her breath.

Then it came in.

"Yes!" Violet said.

"What is that, honey?" It was her mother, suddenly opening her door.

"Can you knock?!"

"What are you so excited about?"

"Nothing."

Her mother wasn't buying it, so she tried to think fast.

"Trevor's coming, that's all," Violet said, and her mother fell at ease, smiling and squeezing Violet's shoulder.

"You really like him, don't you?"

"I guess." Violet was blushing, in front of her mother—the worst.

"Okay, I'll see you down there, honey. You look so pretty in that dress."

The two smiled at each other. Her mother's smile seemed really genuine, but Violet's was tinged with embarrassment and fear.

●  ●  ●

Later that night, on the stairs, with the party in full force above them, the four teens huddled.

Jamie seemed nervous. Sophia too, but she also looked different, happier somehow, or maybe excited. Trevor did too, but he had hunger in his eyes.

Violet spoke first. "We should just confront him. All of us. Get him to talk."

"Yeah," Trevor said. "Strength in numbers."

"What do we say?" Jamie asked.

"We call him on his shit, and we show him the video."

Violet had been waiting for this moment for a long time. She was thankful to have a posse to do it with.

"I'll record the audio," Jamie said.

"Let's do this," Trevor whispered.

The four of them went up the stairs and into the party, hanging out on the outskirts. Someone arrived with a baby, and everyone oohed and aahed. There was a jazz trio in the corner, that was was mostly being ignored. Rent-a-band. Violet couldn't see Lester anywhere, which meant he was probably in his office—hopefully alone.

"Follow me," she said, and off they went.

The fierce foursome.

Or so she hoped.

Lester was, in fact, in his office with the door cracked, talking on the phone. Right in the middle of his own party, which was actually pretty common. He made appearances, but the party was mostly for show.

Violet could literally feel the blood crawling through her veins. She looked at the crew: Trevor was all serious, Sophia kept looking behind her, and Jamie was sweating a little. The three of them nodded in unison, and she opened the door. They walked in slowly, forming a line along one side of his desk. Lester stayed on the phone, first giving them a smile but then realizing this wasn't a playful visit. These were four kids on a mission. He held up his hand and continued to talk.

"End the call, Dickhead," Trevor said under his breath.

Jamie laughed nervously.

They stood there, facing him off, and he backed up a little.

"Okay, gotta run," Lester said, finally hanging up his phone.

"Good thing we can outrun you," Trevor said.

"Well, to what do I owe this pleasure?" Lester crossed his arms, looking at them skeptically.

"We know what you did," Violet said, holding her phone out to him, playing the video.

Lester was trying to act cool, but she could see moisture glistening on his brow. He wiped it with a handkerchief.

Violet continued. "Why in the world would you want to drug someone who worked so hard for you for so many years?"

"Violet, I'm starting to think *you're* on drugs . . ."

"Did he have a secret on you?"

"Who?"

"Brendan, dumbass," Jamie said.

"You watch who you're talking to, you little weasel."

Lester's face turned dark really fast. Violet thought of Ricardo and his warning and thought, *Maybe we should just all get out of there?*

"Violet, what the hell is going on?"

She almost walked away, right then, but when she saw Trevor's glare, his eyes saying *do it, do it*, out came the river of words again.

"Why don't you tell us about the stock JREXX?"

Lester was dumbfounded now. His mouth was open but no words came out, so Violet went on.

"Why would you let Brendan drive after that? Was that your whole plan? He drives into a tree, and you're conveniently rid of him?"

Violet's whole body was pulsing with adrenaline. She had been scared for sure, but now she was just pissed. "Why is it that rich people think they can get away with everything?"

"It's always been like that," Trevor seethed. "Powerful scumbags."

"Where did you get that video?" Lester finally said. "That is invasion of privacy."

"I think you're looking at much more serious charges," Jamie said, his attempt at being menacing turning out to be kind of adorable.

Violet could see Ricardo in the hallway, a phone to his ear, panic on his face. She turned back to Lester, trying to figure out what someone would say on a TV show to get him to talk.

"It's you on the tape. It's blatant evidence."

Lester stepped forward, but no one backed off. In fact, Trevor leaned in.

"Brendan's death was an accident," Lester said. "Now if you'll excuse—"

"It was the perfect murder," Sophia said. No one had expected her to talk, but it stopped the whole room. Everyone stared at her.

Lester smiled, but it looked pained, and he was breathing heavier now.

"You think you've figured it all out, huh?"

"Pretty much," Trevor said.

"What do you want, then?" Lester asked.

There was a long silence that felt really loud; Violet could even hear a ring in her ears. Breaking the spell, Lester pulled open the top drawer of his desk and took out a handgun, laying it on top of the desk. It was jet black and shiny. Violet had never seen a real gun in person before, other than in a policeman's holster.

Jamie gasped, jumping back a little. "What the actual fuck?"

"Look at the weasel now," Lester said.

Violet's mother appeared at the doorway. "What is going on? Lester, the police are here!"

Before anyone could say anything, two officers—one big and one small—gently moved Violet's mother aside and walked into the room.

"Sir, do you have a license for that?" the big cop said, pointing to the gun.

"Of course I do. Do you mind telling me what you're doing in my house?"

"Sir, I need you to calm down. Kids, I need you all out in the hallway. Now."

All four of them gave Lester the evil eye as they walked out. Violet felt a total rush of pride, like she finally did it—she stood up to Lester.

In the hallway, they all started to catch their breath, as if they'd been collectively holding it. Violet could hear the muted sound of the jazz trio still playing under the tent outside.

Sophia turned to Violet and said, "Good job."

"You too."

Jamie and Trevor high-fived.

Ricardo came to ask if they all were all right.

"We are," Violet said, grabbing his arm. "You did the right thing."

They could hear the policeman, the big one, raising his voice, then some kind of shuffle, something being knocked over. Violet's mother let out a squeal.

Trevor got up to go see, and Jamie pulled him back down. "No," he said. "They told us to wait out here."

It went silent for a few moments, and Violet closed her eyes. She didn't pray much, but in that moment, she asked whoever was above to help her mother. To bring Lester to justice so her mother wouldn't get hurt.

A few minutes later, when Lester was escorted past them in handcuffs, some of the partygoers had lined up to watch. Violet's mother followed, giving her a cold, penetrating look, like Violet had betrayed her in a way that could never be forgiven. But Violet was a window. She let her mother's look go right through her.

○ ○ ○

It was midnight, and Violet couldn't sleep. Her mother hadn't returned yet, and she was the only one home . . . except for Ricardo. In her nightgown, she slowly padded down to his room, which had a thin line of light coming through the bottom of the door. Violet put her ear up to it. She heard a whimper. She didn't knock, just opened the door. She knew it was hypocritical, but there were different rules for parents.

He was a mess. His handsome face was all contorted and shiny with remnants of recent tears. She hugged him, saying, "Qué pasa?"

Then she realized. The video. Lester must have known it had come from him.

"Did he fire you?"

"Yes, when he was being arrested. He told me to be gone by the time he was out on bail."

"How did he know?"

"When you guys were in the hallway, they called me in. I couldn't lie to the police."

"Oh, Ricardo, I'm so sorry," Violet said.

Ricardo dabbed at his eyes with a dish towel. "You were right, Babygirl. Lester is a bad man. I've seen a lot of things. That's why I knew something was wrong that night, why I recorded that video." He started laughing, which was odd. "My friend told me I should blackmail him. Te imaginas!"

"Like I said, you did the right thing."

"Is he going to jail?" Ricardo asked.

"Not sure. They got him on the charge of possessing a gun without a license. And they have the video, and my friend Jamie gave them like, a dossier of all the facts."

"Well, I better pack my bags."

"Okay, okay, wait. Hang on a second. Wait right here."

Violet ran upstairs to her room. From the box under her bed, she grabbed the watch her father had given her, which used to be her great-grandmother's. She knew it was worth a lot, but the truth was, she didn't think it was cute at all. She'd never wear it, and she'd never known the woman. She brought it down to the basement, where Ricardo was filling up a bunch of tote bags.

"You won't get a ferry tonight . . ."

"I have a friend I can stay with in mid-island. I'm so sorry, Babygirl."

"I am too." She handed him the watch. "I want you to have this. For everything you've done for us."

Ricardo's watery eyes widened.

"De verdad?"

"Sí, sí."

They hugged, and Violet could smell his leathery cologne. She started to cry.

"Will you say goodbye to your mother for me?"

"Yes. She will be lost without you, though."

"Oh, she'll be ok. It's better that justice is served. Besides, I don't think she liked him as much as she told herself she did. You know what I mean?"

"Yes." Was Violet telling herself she liked Trevor? Would her mother really be okay? The questions swirled around her head like tiny flying insects. She dabbed at her eyes with the sleeve of her dress.

"Tell her she can call me anytime."

"I'm sure she will."

Ricardo grabbed the rest of his things from the top of his desk: rosary beads, a framed picture of his nieces, several bottles of vitamins. All in all, he had very little, and it gave Violet a hollow feeling. Now he wouldn't even have a job. She hadn't really thought of that repercussion.

"Maybe if something happens with my music I can hire you back?"

Ricardo smiled and kissed Violet on her cheek.

They went upstairs. An Uber was waiting for him in the driveway. They each had tears in their eyes as they hugged one last time, and then he turned and walked down the drive.

She shut the door, turned around, and sighed, looking around the kitchen, which already seemed empty without Ricardo. But there was someone there—a new person. For a second she braced herself. Was it an intruder? Was Lester back, about to reach out and strangle her? But she only sighed again. It was Trevor.

"Sorry to startle you. I was wondering . . . I didn't want you to be alone. Do you want to stay with me tonight?"

It was a simple question, and so was her answer.
"Yes."

○ ○ ○

Two houses down, on the second floor of a guest cottage, Trevor's room looked directly out onto the Atlantic, which at that hour she could see only by the light of the half-moon. His room was in disarray, and he started frantically cleaning everything up. What was it about boys and just piling stuff on the floor? Still, it was cute watching him, like he was doing it for her sake. After he finished tidying, he got an air mattress out of his closet and plugged it in. As it blew up, he walked right up next to her. The noise from the pump was really loud, but she felt calm. His eyes were the color of sun-bleached blueberries; she'd never noticed that before. His lips were slightly parted, and she wanted to kiss him, but she froze. The pump got louder as the mattress filled. He unplugged it and said, "I can sleep on this. You take the bed."

This time she walked up to him. Real close.

"I don't mind sharing."

He smiled and gently pulled the pencil out of her hair. Then he kissed her, and she finally knew what that *thing* felt like. The tiny bursts of light. The tingling. The sped up heart. All of it was happening. He tasted a little sweet. Was it chocolate? She touched the skin on his arms, which was incredibly smooth.

They parted and stared at each other, smiling. He was the most handsome guy she'd ever kissed, that was for sure.

On his bed, clothes still on, she used his chest as a pillow. She could hear his muted heartbeat thumping underneath his

T-shirt, which had an intoxicating scent of detergent mixed with a little sweat.

"You okay?" Trevor asked.

"Never better."

After a while, they heard the front door slam, followed by someone walking up the stairs.

"I heard what happened. You okay in there?" came his mother's voice from the hallway.

"Fine, Ma," Trevor said, squeezing Violet, the two of them softly giggling. "Gonna get some rest," Trevor added.

After his mother went back downstairs and back to the main house, Violet said, "I'm really glad you blew up that air mattress."

"Well, I didn't want to assume . . ."

"You know, I used to call you Pretty Boy?"

"I know."

She lifted up her head and kissed him once, softly, then said, "But you're more than just a pretty face. I see that now."

"I'm glad." He moved his hair out of his eyes and took a deep breath. "This is going to sound weird, but when you were confronting Lester, it was totally sexy."

"Sexy?"

"Yes. Am I allowed to say that? You were so confident, so strong. It was hot."

"So you're saying confident girls are hot?"

"Yes."

"Well, so are confident guys. I was thinking the same thing about you."

Their bodies seemed to melt together, as if they were merging into one person. Where did she end and he begin? Could that be a song lyric, or was that too cheesy?

They breathed at the same rhythm, maybe even thinking the same thoughts. She never knew it could be this way, that it could feel this right.

She hoped it wasn't just because of everything that had happened that night. She suddenly became incredibly tired. She thought of texting her mother, but it would have to wait.

For now, she would fall asleep in the arms of a beautiful boy.

# CHAPTER 15

# JAMIE

He knew Trevor and Violet were going to hook up, and he was happy for them. Better than Trevor and Sophia. Even though Trevor seemed different, he could still be a bad influence on her. Or maybe Jamie was still hoping he had a chance with Sophia, in case it didn't work out with Cameron? He had definitely been obsessed with her. But who was he kidding? With Cameron it was like trying a food he'd never tasted and instantly knowing it would be his favorite.

At his catering gig the next day, he felt lighter on his feet. He texted Cameron when he had a break.

*Looks like we caught the bad guy*

*That's excellent! How are you feeling?*

*Like I'm a couple inches above the ground*

*Not a bad place to be*

There was a pause, where both of them were typing. Bubbles appearing and disappearing. He wanted to tell Cameron that he missed him, but he felt like a boy with a dumb crush. Cameron seemed to hear his thoughts, as the next text asked Jamie if he'd like to come to Boston the following week to visit him.

Jamie had to force himself to delay his answer, which was eventually a yes in all caps. He followed it up with, *What do I wear?*

*I'm thinking sequins?*

*Ha. Not me.*

*I know. Just bring yourself. And some clothes of course.*☺

Jamie almost typed *ones that easily come off?* but went for *I'll bring my best T-shirt* instead.

*That works. We can go to the aquarium.*

Now it was sounding like a date. He refrained from typing a fact about marine mammals—he would save it. He just typed, *Can't wait.*

After reading a couple unread texts from Violet, he learned that Lester was out on bail, but thankfully already in New York. Something about damage control. The whole island was talking about him, and Jamie felt like a celebrity, especially with his boss, Pete, who walked up to him just then.

"You guys are heroes," Peter said. "This island will have one less douchebag."

"It was pretty awesome. The guy was squirming."

Jamie thought of those charged moments. How their collective intimidation and power shut Lester down. It was invigorating, even if the guy called him a weasel. Sticks and stones . . .

"Is the stepdaughter still there?" Pete wanted to know.

"Violet? Yes, but her mother told Lester he can't come back until the deposition."

"Let's just hope he doesn't throw his goons on you."

"What?"

Jamie was finally able to breathe. Now he had to worry about goons?

"Just kidding," Pete said. "Even that guy wouldn't stoop so low to mess with a bunch of teenagers."

"I'm not going to stress. I just want to *be* a teenager."

Pete laughed and gave him a friendly punch on his arm.

"You're a good kid. Now get back to work."

After his shift, he rode his bike by Low Beach where he'd first hung out with Violet, which seemed like a lifetime ago. A young couple was walking their dog, laughing. Some kids were playing in the sand. The world seemed somehow restored.

When he got back to the cottage, his aunt Gia made him his favorite sandwich—turkey and provolone on sourdough. It tasted like heaven. While eating it, he realized that for a long time, he hadn't really enjoyed food. Now the knots that had plagued his stomach were loosened, twisted free.

"You seem really happy today," Gia said.

Jamie had been in touch with his parents, but besides Cameron, he really hadn't told anyone what was going on. He knew Gia wouldn't judge him, so he just started talking. He told her everything, from the eggs to Lester drugging Brendan to Ricardo calling the police.

"Well, my whole drama this summer has been some flooding in the basement. Looks like you beat me on that. Have you told your mom?"

"No! She gets really protective. Can we not tell her?"

"Sure."

Jamie went to straighten the whale-shaped salt and pepper shakers but then just let them be. Gia smiled.

"So, I'm gonna go to Boston this weekend to visit my friend Cameron."

"Okay. What about telling your mom that?"

"I'd rather not."

"Is this a romantic thing?"

Because of the way she asked the question, as if it was totally normal, Jamie answered the same way.

"Not sure. Maybe."

Gia smiled and said, "Great. Just be safe, and check in with me."

"Cool."

Jamie loved adults like Gia. Ones who didn't blow things out of proportion, who seemed more like friends than people who were always trying to give advice and keep him in some kind of box. In that moment, he was extremely grateful for Gia.

"Thanks, you know, for everything," Jamie said.

Gia took his sandwich plate and said, "I'm here all week."

When the day finally came to visit Cameron, Jamie was more relieved than nervous. He found that once he was under Cameron's spell, he was comfortable. It was the waiting that made him anxious.

On the ferry, Jamie checked in with his parents. His mother said she missed him, and it was nice to be missed. He actually missed her too, although he also felt his own independence growing inside him at a rate beyond his control.

He got off the ferry and onto the bus to South Station, then got an Uber to Cameron's place in Cambridge. It was a second-floor apartment with Tibetan prayer flags over the door. Cameron let him in, and they sat in the living room. There was a giant poster of David Bowie on the wall and a bunch of mannequins in various states of dress scattered around the room.

"My roommate, Reece, is a fashion designer. Someday he'll dress actual people."

"I heard that," said a tall, skinny guy walking out of his bedroom wearing what looked like a Japanese robe. "I'm Reece. Hi, Cutie."

Jamie hoped his face was just red and not purple. He'd never been called a "cutie" by a guy before—although he wasn't so sure if "guy" was the appropriate term, as Reece was clearly transitioning. Jamie tried to act cool. Just because you weren't used to something didn't mean you had to be alienated by it. If there's one thing Jamie had learned this summer, it was to not make assumptions based on the surface. What you see of people on the outside is only the beginning. For all he knew, Reece was a black belt in karate. Well, maybe not, but you never knew.

The three of them talked about Jamie's trip and the weather. It felt to Jamie like an adult conversation. When Reece left, Cameron moved closer on the couch. Jamie couldn't believe it. He was in a college student's apartment, about to have sex. Well, he hoped so . . .

The night didn't go exactly as planned. At first, it was just the two of them. Cameron spoke about the novel he was writing, which was about a troubled girl on the streets of Las Vegas who gets involved in a murder. Sounded familiar. Jamie told him that he "came out" to his aunt, or so he thought. Cameron listened with earnestness, taking Jamie's hand and lightly petting it.

Just when Jamie thought they were going to kiss, Reece came back, with two friends and a bottle of vodka. A party ensued. They did a shot, which Jamie had to pretend he was used to. It stung his throat like crazy. He never liked to drink much, but tonight, when the burn went away, he felt it warming his blood.

As the evening progressed, Jaime secretly noticed how at ease Cameron was with everyone. He already had an agent for his novel. He was smart, successful, in school, together—and he was gay. The whole thing felt revealing to Jamie then, as if up until that point he'd been living in black and white and now everything was in bright color. He was no longer that scared kid in eighth grade, sitting in the corner alone at the dance. He was in the dance now. He *was* the dance.

They played charades and then that raunchy card game everyone was playing. Then Reece put on some house music, the good kind with melody, and Cameron grabbed Jamie to dance with him. It was the first time that he could remember dancing without being self-conscious. Jamie skipped the next round of shots. He was so happy, he wanted to stay in the same exact mood.

The party eventually died down, and they all watched a movie. Jamie fell asleep against Cameron's shoulder, completely embarrassed when he woke and saw his drool on Cameron's shirt. But Cameron just laughed, leading Jamie into his bedroom, where they both stripped off everything but their underwear—Cameron in boxers, Jamie in briefs. They got into bed and embraced, skin on skin, and Jamie felt like he might just explode. Was he holding this back his whole life? Was it guys that he liked, or was it just Cameron? Whatever, there was no stopping him. They kissed and explored each other's bodies with their hands. At one point Cameron got on top of him, and Jamie's brain was scrambling. What position was he supposed to be? He barely knew anything about this! Cameron, sensing Jamie's panic, told him they would take it slow, just be together tonight. So that's what they did. And it didn't feel wrong or shameful. It just felt wonderful.

In the courtroom, Jamie sat in between Trevor and Sophia.

Violet was in the row behind them, with her mother.

Lester had taken a plea deal, and the sentence was going to be announced.

Somewhere, deep down, Jamie had always thought a few eggs causing someone to drive into a tree seemed a little far-fetched—but it was possible, and seemed true at the time. However, Operation Freedom was now about to succeed. It was crazy that one stupid thing they did changed their lives in the blink of an eye.

When they announced Lester's sentence—fourteen months in medium-security prison—Trevor let out his signature whoop.

Violet was consoling her mother, who was softly crying.

Lester looked at Jamie, his eyes piercing from all the way across the room. A man scorned. Jamie stared right back at him, a slight smile on his face. *Who's the weasel now?* he thought.

The video wasn't enough to prove Lester had drugged Brendan (the attorney claimed he was putting bitters into the glass, to make a drink called an old-fashioned), but Lester pleaded guilty to insider trading and to possession of an illegal drug. The gun charge was thrown out.

As they walked out of the courtroom into the bright sunlight, Jamie thought back to first meeting Trevor and Sophia, in the parking lot of the movie theater. Who could have guessed they would go through all this in such a short period of time.

The three of them hugged each other, and Trevor went off to find Violet.

"So, J, how was your Boston trip?" Sophia asked.

Jamie just smiled. He didn't need to say anything.

"Well, at least someone's getting some," she said.

As they walked down the steps, Jamie's phone buzzed. It was a text from Cameron. Every time he saw the name, his heart did a little dance.

*How'd it go?*

*Jail time,* Jamie texted back.

Cameron sent four thumbs-up emojis.

Jamie started to respond but noticed Cameron was still texting.

He waited until it finally came through.

One red heart.

The day before he left the island, Jamie took a long walk along Sconset beach. He knew Violet was the only one in their group left on the island and that she was working on her music and helping her mother, who was not taking the whole scandal very well, as expected.

As Jamie got closer, he could see Violet on the stairs, just like the first time they met, except this time her hair was down and there was a large man next to her. For a second, Jamie worried that it was Lester, but the man had a darker complexion. As soon as she saw Jamie, Violet waved him up.

He hugged her. In fact, they had all been hugging each other more after the whole thing went down. Solidarity. When they broke apart, Violet turned to the man and said, "Jamie, this is my father. Dad, this is Jamie."

Her father's hands were rough, but his eyes were kind.

"So, you came back?" Jamie said.

He nodded and smiled. The two of them were beaming—so much so, that Jamie felt like he was intruding on something super personal.

"Okay, I'm going to keep walking. I just wanted to say bye."

"Until next summer?" Violet asked.

"Until next summer."

Jamie walked back down the stairs, and this time took his shoes off. He walked back through the surf, his shoes dangling from his right hand.

Everything wasn't so complicated anymore. Well, it was, but he was different now. He was excited to start his senior year. The *New Yorker* had passed on his piece about his neighbor Grace but gave him two suggestions for where to try and publish it. He was hopeful.

One of his favorite animal facts, which he had told Cameron at the aquarium, was that sea otters hold hands when they sleep so they don't drift away from each other. He had spent many sleepless nights in a bed made of ocean, drifting alone, wondering where he'd end up. A lonely and lost sea otter. Now he felt connected to the world—especially after getting his two best friends back. It was a long shot, but maybe Cameron would be that sea otter. The one he'd see in the morning, the one who would have his back while he floated through unknown waters.

# ONE YEAR LATER

The four teens are eating ice cream on a bench downtown. Tourists roll their suitcases awkwardly down the cobblestone sidewalks of Main Street, some sunburned, some tired, some just sad looking. It's the end of another summer, a summer where mostly good things happened this time. Trevor taught Violet how to surf, and she taught him how to sail. They also taught each other things between the sheets. He made a tire swing for Bryce. He even played golf with his father.

Violet is on one end of the bench, eating a cup of mint chocolate chip. She keeps checking her phone.

"Anything?" Trevor asks.

"Nope."

She is waiting to hear back from Meghan Trainor's manager, who had finally agreed to listen to her tracks.

Her phone dings, but it's her dad, who has moved back from California. He spent the summer with Violet and her mom, who moved out of Lester's house to their old cottage in Surfside.

Violet stares at the text and smiles.

"That's my dad. Normally I'd roll my eyes at a parental text, but it's so nice having him around."

Trevor kisses her forehead.

"You know, even though my parents sleep in separate rooms,

every so often I see them glance at each other fleetingly, something sharp in their eyes."

"And you're keeping track of them."

"Yeah, I guess. I just wonder what it would take for them to pull together again."

"Anything can happen," Trevor says.

Violet has her own pulling going on. For a while now. A pull toward a certain surfer sitting next to her.

On the other side of Trevor, Sophia licks her cone of vanilla with rainbow sprinkles. Some of the little colorful bits stick to her cheek. She is happy. Junior year had been cool. She killed her grades, took Letisha to see Lizzo, and got to play violin at Carnegie Hall with her school choir. She hung out with Jamie and Trevor pretty regularly, when they weren't in Boston with Cameron and Violet, respectively.

*One more year*, she keeps telling herself. She already has a Pinterest page with all her dorm furniture ideas for Brown. She manifested getting in, so much so that she didn't really have a backup plan, aside from one state school. Before getting her acceptance letter, she jokingly told her mothers that if she didn't get in she was going to surf Costa Rica with Trevor. They didn't think that was very funny.

There was one thing she did during the summer that felt kind of epic, to her at least. She went home to Connecticut with her moms for a visit, and while getting some frozen yogurt with Letisha, she noticed someone familiar across the way, on the Starbucks patio. Something about the tilt of the guy's head . . . then she saw the purple water bottle, and it hit her: it was Lyle, her former violin teacher, sitting with a girl even younger than

Sophia. When he went inside, Sophia told Letisha to stay put, and then she walked across to their table.

"Hey, how do you know Lyle?"

"Oh, he's my violin teacher. Why?"

"'Cause he was mine too. Until he wasn't."

"What do you mean?"

"I mean, he's a perv. You should find another teacher."

"Really?"

"Really."

The girl seemed stunned. She slowly stood up and walked away.

Sophia went back to her table at the yogurt place.

"What was that about?" Letisha asked.

"Just some fair warning."

As they finished their yogurt, Sophia watched Lyle come back with two drinks, looking around for the girl, squinting his eyes. Finally, he sat down, shaking his head. Sophia started giggling. She couldn't help it. Letisha did too, if only because it was contagious.

Now, watching the summer people line up for the ferry, it feels like everything is on track. But Sophia knows better. Tracks weren't straight, and life was a crooked game. She just had to play hard, play fair, and hope for the best.

On the other side of Sophia, Jamie points to her cheek.

"Are you saving those for later?"

Sophia brushed the sprinkles off, saying, "Very funny."

Jamie is reading something on his phone, and Sophia asks him what it is.

"It's the first chapter of Cameron's novel."

"Cool. What's it like?"

"It's a little over the top, but very . . . vivid. He's pretty talented."

"As are you. I read that piece you did on your neighbor."

Jamie waves her off, but his eyes glow.

"I never asked you," Sophia says. "How was it, coming out to your parents?"

Jamie puts his phone down and sips his peanut butter shake.

"It was way easier than I thought. My father cringed a little, but my mom just hugged me and said, 'Love whoever you want to, but I want to meet him.'"

Sophia smiles. On the other end of the bench, Violet leans her head onto Trevor's shoulder, the two of them in their own world.

"So did she? Get to meet him?"

"Yes. She liked him."

"You don't sound very enthused."

"Well, I'm trying to be realistic. He's my first guy, so I can't be like, running off into the sunset with him."

Sophia smiles and says, "Makes sense."

"What about you? Any romantic prospects?"

"No, just Bailey."

Jamie giggles.

"You've always loved that dog."

After the four of them finish, they get up and start walking back toward Trevor's Jeep.

The sky is an electric blue, and the late afternoon sun shoots pinpoints of light through the leaves of the ancient oak trees that line Main Street.

They walk lightly, no longer followed by a dark, heavy cloud.

They are free.

# ACKNOWLEDGEMENTS

I am grateful for the island of Nantucket, which has always felt like home to me. Its awe-inspiring beauty, colorful people, and way of casting a spell. I've always wanted to set a book there, and I hope I've done it justice.

Thank you:

To my agent, Christopher Schelling, for always encouraging and believing in me.

To Alice Randall, for her generosity and kindness.

To Stephanie Beard and everyone at Turner Publishing, I'm honored to join the family.

To Carole Heaton and Michael Morrow, whose widow's walk inspired my opening scene, and who remain some of the coolest people on Baxter Road.

To my husband Steve Swenson, for always reading drafts, and having my back. I honestly couldn't do it without you.

# ABOUT THE AUTHOR

Stewart Lewis has published six novels, including *You Have Seven Messages*, which has been translated into five languages. He is a professor at Belmont University, and a singer songwriter whose songs have been placed in TV and Film worldwide. For more information, visit www.stewartlewis.com.